Spirit of the Sandhills

by Harry Norval

with Julie Liska

This book is a work of fiction. Places, events, and situations in this story are purely fictional. Any resemblance to actual persons, living or dead, is coincidental.

ISBN: 0-7596-5385-2

This book is printed on acid free paper.

1stBooks - rev. 2/15/02

Dedication

This book is dedicated to my parents Harry and Millie Norval – and also to my wife Bruni Norval.

This story came to be written as the result of my wifes fascination with the Sandhills area of Nebraska. Bruni was born and raised in Berlin, Germany. Following World War II she became a U.S. citizen and settled in Nebraska. She became intrigued with the Sandhill area of the state — what a contrast to anything she'd ever been exposed to before. Although we did not live in the Sandhill area of the state, the stories of success and broken dreams from this area lead us to discover one either loves or despises this vast land — thus this story developed.

Thanks to Julie Liska for reviewing and making suggestions to the story — Spirit of the Sandhills.

Chapter 1

Spring filled the air that Sunday afternoon in 1943 as a warm sun teased life from Nebraska's greening prairie. The heavy smell of damp, winter ravaged soil was fading. In it's place was a new scent—that of something light and sweet. Drifting on the wings of a mild southern breeze was a mixture of freshly cut hay and blooming clover. As frail white puffs trailed across the bright blue sky, a shy wind whispered quietly to all who would listen. A new season was beginning. A season full of hope and a promise of better things to come.

Filled with unbridled enthusiasm, the sun's persistent rays broke through the windows of North Platte high school, illuminating those gathered. But despite the days hopeful promise, those seated in the auditorium appeared oblivious.

The 30 young men and women seated in anticipation of receiving high school diplomas were actually doing much more. As they prepared to bid their high school farewell, so too would pass their youthful innocence. It was a time of war and a country in need was calling out. The soon-to-be graduates of safe, secure North Platte High School would be expected to answer that call.

Among them was John Olson. Strikingly tall and muscular, the dark-haired rancher's son had called western Nebraska home for 18 years. His back yard was a rolling sandhill prairie that bristled with native prairie grasses swaying in the breeze.

As he sat in a hard, wooden chair John listened as the valedictorians final farewell chant drifted through the air. Glancing down, John eyed his neatly-folded hands. Their callouses confessed to years of hot summer days spent making fence. Gathering his fingers into a fist, he recalled long days of working cattle alongside his father. Bringing the beasts in from pasture with horses, roping them, and even the sickly smell of flesh scorched by the icy-hot flame of a branding iron were things John knew well. Things he enjoyed and could predict. Things he knew could soon be coming to an end.

Glancing up, John watched as bits of dust danced in the suns warm glow. Despite the joyous appearance of the day, his heart was heavy. Many young men from the area had already been drafted, and no end to the need was in sight. Those now seated around him in wait of their

1

diplomas were actually facing a life-altering decision. All the young men—John's childhood chums—would next find themselves registering for the draft. Most surely some would end up overseas, fighting for their country in a foreign land.

As the high school principal took the podium John noticed, for the first time, how the smell of chalk dust lingered in the air.

"Perhaps," he thought, "I am already assuming the role of manhood." Why else would a smell he grew up with, and be oblivious to for years, suddenly become so obvious?

Did his classmates notice it? Did they notice the subtle change that had taken place among them even as this rite of passage progressed? A few seats down, John stole a glance at Pete Mill, a good friend since grade school.

John reflected on time spent with his good friend. When younger, both participated in events at county fair, where they competed to show the best 4-H heifer. Gradually they changed into Saturday nights at the movie theater, a game of pool, trips to the rodeo and scraping up what little bit of spending money they had to buy a bottle of home brew. The memories fell together like the pieces of a complicated jigsaw puzzle. They were good times, the kind shared between friends over the course of years.

A sideways glance at another buddy, Justin Temple, reminded him of long evenings spent getting stubborn Model T Ford running. As time passed, others had joined in. They eventually became a close-knit group of friends.

Working on a Model A Ford had become their next project. Weeks passed as adjustments were made and the old car finally relented, purring softly in gratitude at their efforts. Showing off their accomplishments, the friends got together, hot rodding down country roads and sparse North Platte streets.

John thought back on the many conversations he had with his friends and classmates as they worked on their hobby. While honing their mechanical expertise, talk drifted to other subjects—livestock, school and even girls. But in the last year, almost every conversation was dominated by the discussion of war and what impact it would have on their lives.

As the small school band brought instruments to their lips in preparation for a final farewell, John caught a glimpse of his parents in the audience. His mother Helen was dressed in a blue dress dotted with hundreds of overlapping daises. Her face seemed relaxed and pleasant, enjoying this landmark event in her only sons life.

While she had the air of a young woman, deeply-etched lines around her eyes and mouth told of difficult times spent on the open prairie. Her childhood had been spent on the sand hills. The daughter of sturdy pioneers, she had grown up seeing hardship and succeeding despite the obstacles life presented. Working hard was a way of life Helen learned at her mother's knee and embraced throughout her lifetime.

Seated next to Helen was John's father Ed, a large, strong man who, like his wife, spent a lifetime working hard. He had survived the drought and depression of the dirty '30's. With the help and support of his wife, he cajoled a living from the fickle Nebraska soil year after year. In the process, Ed became highly regarded by the community. A steadfast faith in God was his beacon in life, and each Sunday the Olson's could be found in the tiny country church located just down the road.

The Olson's goal was to raise a son, both strong and capable. One who would grow up to be like his ancestors. A survivor who knew what hard work meant and wouldn't be afraid to take life head-on, just like his parents and grandparents had done before him.

Now in his 50's, Ed was looking forward to having some relief from work's constant demands. John's skill on the ranch, learned through many seasons, was needed. His full-time help after graduation, a long-anticipated possibility, was finally close to becoming a reality.

As the only child of a rancher, the option of seeking a hardship deferment existed. Taking advantage of the service waiver would enable John to stay home and assist his parents despite the war. But that desire was balanced by the forced recruitment of so many of John's friends, and the cries of a country in need.

So the family's hopes of John staying on the ranch dimmed as he and his fellow graduates prepared to leave North Platte High School. Exiting the auditorium, John felt the ghost of childhood linger behind, trapped in a time and place inaccessible except in a fleeting memory. Striding forward, John mentally bid farewell to the young boy he was leaving behind.

As graduates, parents and friends stood sharing enthusiastic hugs, handshakes and pats on the back, John sensed a new presence entering the scene—a replacement for the essence of youth being left behind. Bracing slightly, but with little regret, John set his sights on the demands of adulthood baying anxiously in the distance.

***

"Foolish, foolish workmen," Agnes Morris pouted, her thin, brightly-painted pink lips pursed in disgust.

"What could have they been thinking, leaving this shoddy looking azalea in my front garden for all to see? Everybody knows a person's true worth is evident from the looks of their entry. Well, I just have no recourse but to go over Maurice's head about this."

Agnes was directing her complaints to pretty 18-year-old Sarah who stood listening, eyes rolling upwards.

"Mother, really. It's just one sickly-looking plant. Watch this."

Sarah unceremoniously peeled a pair of white dress gloves from her hands, thrusting them at Agnes. Gathering her billowing, calf-length skirt in one hand she ventured off the freshly-swept sidewalk, half-burying her spotless white pumps in the gardens tacky soil. In a single fluid motion Sara grabbed hold of the flowers stem,uprooted it, and stuffed it behind a nearby shrub. Without pausing Sara then popped back onto the sidewalk.

"There you go, mother. No more pesky azalea to trouble yourself with."

With hands resting on narrow hips, Agnes' brow furrowed. Even her perfectly coiffed hair, fixed in a style suitable for afternoon tea, appeared to stiffen indignantly.

"Oh, really, Sara. Do you think that was necessary?"

"Yes mother, I do. Now, if you excuse me, I have a few things to do in my room."

Grabbing her white gloves from Agnes' hand she turned to go. The mother's disapproving frown followed Sara up the steps. Pushing open the heavy oak entry door, the young girl flew past expensive, antique vases flanking the entryway and made her way up a grand, arching staircase.

Once in her bedroom, Sarah tossed her things down on the bed and headed for the vanity. Collapsing into a gracefully embroidered chair, she began fiddling restlessly with an attached tassel. Absentmindedly, her eyes drifted to the vanity mirror.

Framed within it's golden scrolls was a fair-skinned girl with layers of dark brown curls encircling a heart-shaped face. Her small, strawberry-shaped mouth looked as if it could burst into laughter at any moment. Above her pert nose were green eyes with dramatic, arching brows, They gave the appearance of barely hiding the amusement the world so readily offered.

But today, that spirit was clouded. Staring at the mirrors image, Sara began to grimace.

"What in the world am I doing here?," she asked herself. On brief hiatus from her exclusive New England preparatory school, Sara had returned to her parents vast Hidden Valley estate.

But since arriving home, she and her mother were constantly at odds. Both strong-willed, Sara had always bent to accommodate her mother's social proddings. For years she had endured endless afternoons at the club, where the height of embarrassment was to fail a test of etiquette before her mother's captious acquaintances. It was a place where saying just the right thing, or being associated with just the right people could mean the difference between being accepted — or being deemed a pitiful outcast merely tolerated for the groups amusement.

The pressure to succeed in this competitive social environment was always there, brought home and enforced by her overzealous mother. It crept into almost every aspect of her life, affecting the organizations Sara participated in, the schools she went to and even the small circle of people she called friends.

The only relief was her father, Joseph. An easy-going, happy man in his early 50's, he seemed blissfully oblivious to the world his wife so purposefully orchestrated. He would accompany his family to weekly garden parties or afternoon clay shoots, his easy-going laugh flowing easily. Trading in his legal briefs for a polo shirt and loose-fitting slacks, the man with salt-and-pepper hair would discount his peers mean-spirited undertones. He enjoyed seeing the good in people, and accepted them as they were.

And this made Sara love him dearly, for it meant that he accepted her, too. There were no critical underpinnings in their relationship. Just an appreciation for each other and the understanding that being human is inexplicably connected to fallibility.

Sara pulled herself up and walked to a book shelf across the room. Running her fingers over the spines, she felt as though she were visiting old friends. In the quiet, solitary days of her youth she had spent hours lost between their covers. They had introduced her to colorful people who had no need for the complicated masks those surrounding her needed. Within them, new worlds unfolded. And Sara was surprised to realize there was a different universe outside her own. One far removed from that of ladies clubs and high school galas.

Within a month, she would be graduating. Sara's mouth pursed as she remembered the early-summer holiday her mother planned. Oh yes, there was a war going on, Sara knew. But the whole thing seemed quite distant—like a shadow luring in the daylight hours.

Sometimes she would overhear the men, gathered about in a businesslike manner, critiquing the Allies progress. And the women, congregated around white linen tables on sunlit verandas, would discuss in hushed tones the names of relatives and distant friends who were involved in the war effort.

Despite the world's events, Agnes had continued to suggest— demand, actually— the family get away before Sara left for college. Despite Joseph's initial objections, he eventually gave in to his wife's request.

"Great," Sara breathed to herself. "More teas and dinner parties. All the same people except with different names."

One thing Sara was sure of were her plans after graduation. She loved children and recognized the value of education. Despite her mother's proddings to stay near home and entertain plans for marriage and children, Sara refused to be deterred from dream of being a teacher. And should that fail, she would still have a minor in business to fall back on. Through her fathers acquaintances, Sara knew well how the business world worked.

Staring blankly out her bedroom window, Sara noted that within the last few days the landscape began showing shades of green. A large old sycamore tree outside her window was on the verge of making a grand entrance in springs supple green attire.

Sara reflected on her life. No, she was not a straight "A" student. But she was sure her solid B average would carry her through college. And once her goal was obtained, then what?

Sara had a hard time envisioning her life in the future. She saw her life flip by, like the fresh pages of a new novel. But there were many unwritten pages in Sara Morris' life. Eventually their contents would become known. For now, though, in her youthful anticipation, the curiosity to imagine what lay ahead was a burden that could only be lessened by the passage of life.

***

Days passed, and John's fears were realized as friends, acquaintances and relatives enlisted in the armed forces and were swept away to far flung places a ranchers son could only imagine. Some entered the military service to avoid being drafted, others out of loyalty, and some out of ignorance. Torn, the young North Platte native decided to seek his father's council on what he should do.

Once asked, John was sure his father would tell him to remain at the ranch.

After a morning of work, John seized his chance. As the duo finished pitching hay to a group of young heifers, Ed paused to guzzle water from a worn jug. Setting it down, he slapped his dusty, patched jeans and rested a foot on a whitened stump. Crossing his hands across a knee, Ed studied the animals before him.

Using a sleeve to wipe gritty sweat off his brow, John joined his father, gingerly approaching the question of his future.

"Dad, I've been thinking a lot about what I should do—enlist, or stay around here to help out. What's your opinion?," he said. Barely breathing, John rested his foot upon the same stump and searched his father's face.

Ed's brow furrowed deeply beneath the shadow of his worn cowboy hat. With a quick push of a gloved hand, he tapped the brim back, exposing slate-blue eyes. Pausing for a moment, he gathered his thoughts.

"Well, son, there comes a time when we all have to make our own decisions. And it looks like this is your time. You'll have to use your own judgment on this, and deal with the hand that's dealt you."

John continued standing there, his even expression masking surprise. Although it was not what he'd expected to hear, John knew it was the truth. Taking his foot off the worn old tree, John stood upright, pausing for a moment before turning toward home.

The next few days flew by. For John, it was a time of turmoil and indecision. On Friday, he found himself headed for Justin Temple's home, just as he had done so many times before. When he got there, he was surprised to see a group of friends gathered outside the barn, visiting lazily around an old car.

"What do you say?," Justin shouted as he caught sight of John approaching.

"Oh, not much. Looks like everyone's got the same idea this evening," John said motioning to those gathered around.

"Well, it turns out this is a kind of farewell party. Looks as if I'll be on the next train headed for California."

John stood in shock for a moment, unable to grasp the full consequences of his friends remark.

"Yep, looks like the U.S. military can use another old country boy," Justin continued. "I decided to go ahead and enlist so I could pick the branch of service I wanted. And it looks like this boy's going to sea," he said, punctuating his words with a jaunty salute.

Philip Dye, a friend known for his quick wit, thumped Justin on the back firmly.

"Looks like our friend didn't want to leave things to chance and end up on latrine detail," Philip said with a chuckle.

As the evening progressed, the close-knit group bantered back and forth, exchanging stories of brothers, sisters, friends and close relatives whose lives were put on hold by the wars many demands. John listened intently, all the while weighing the options in his mind. Go or stay — security or honor — war or family. The answer in his heart was clear. But, there was so much more to consider.

John continued to ponder throughout the evening and much of the next day. Finally, as he and his parents gathered for their evening meal the following day, he felt as if it was time to make his decision known.

As his parents said grace, John noticed the many gray hair peppering his parents bowed heads. The burdens of many seasons showed in their gently draped shoulders. Relentlessly, times strain was taking a toll — the duty of living more difficult with each passing day.

Fiddling with the food on his dinner plate, John discovered the warm, rich scent of roast beef and smothered mashed potatoes had little appeal. Taking a deep breath and grasping his fork tightly, the young man cleared his throat.

"Mom, Dad, I want you to know I've given this a lot of thought. In fact, it's almost all I've been able to think about. But it just looks like I need to go ahead and join the service. I just don't feel right seeking a deferment, and I guess I want to do something before my number comes up with the draft board."

Grabbing the corner of her apron, John's mother dabbed the corner of her eye and seemed to crumple before his eyes. But her weakness lasted only a few moments, replaced almost immediately with a look of determination. It was the look John had seen from his mother many times when hope seemed lost, but faith assertively stepped in to counter.

"I've decided to go ahead and enlist in the Navy. It looks like that might be the safest bet right now," John said looking from parent to parent.

"If you've decided, then we will abide by your wishes," Ed said, pursing his lips and nodding his head in affirmation. Then, as an afterthought added, "Just remember — don't volunteer for anything."

Chapter 2

A whirl of activity took place over the next few days. A quick response from the military solidified John's plans to join the Navy. Papers instructed the 18-year-old North Platte boy to report to the Omaha recruitment office. From there, he would travel to Manhattan Beach, Sheepshead Bay, New York for basic training.

Three days before his scheduled arrival in New York, John and his father set out for the 250-mile trip to Omaha, where his journey would begin. It would be the longest journey the 18-year-old had ever made.

Dressed in jeans and a casual, loose-fitting shirt, John knew it wouldn't be long before his familiar clothes were replaced with Navy garb. Throwing a duffel into the back seat of his father's dusty 1940 Chevrolet, John slipped into the passenger seat. His father slowly guided the car down the long, narrow driveway. With an ache, John felt all he knew become more and more distant with each passing mile.

As the car's tires hit the highway and reached a top speed of 45 miles per hour, John and his father exchanged an occasional comment. Ed pointed out some winter wheat making a grand spring entrance. John remarked lightly on a group of cattle grazing by the roadside. Both knew the sparse conversation was masking the unsettled doubts each was struggling with.

A storm of emotion was masked by John's calm countenance. His mind became more clouded with doubt as the roadside flickered by. How could he have been so foolish to leave his parents and the only lifestyle he ever knew? What was he headed for? Questions and admonitions grew, mudding John's thoughts. But he gradually began to accept the fact his anxious questions would beg answers until time saw fit to make everything clear.

Six hours later, the two pulled into the Omaha train station. The sight that greeted John was difficult for him to comprehend. People sharing exuberant hellos were sprinkled among others bidding tearful farewells. Military personnel, dressed in official attire were scattered about, sleeping on benches or on the floor awaiting their train's arrival.

As John got closer he watched as a car full of military personnel rumbled across the rails. Off in a corner, a military man barked orders to a group of men bound in handcuffs. Flanked by gun-toting guards, John assumed they were captured German soldiers. They were no doubt destined for one of the rural Nebraska prison camps set up that purpose.

The scene of chaotic emotion stunned John, who had never traveled much beyond the borders of his own home town. Fear over making a mistake by enlisting began to burn in his stomach. In amazement, he turned to his father who was also viewing the scene in astonishment.

After the right train was located, John smiled weakly at his father. The time for saying goodbye had arrived all too quickly. With a brisk hug the two exchanged heartfelt farewells. Before turning to go, Ed gave one more piece of advice.

"Just remember what I said, son. Don't volunteer for anything."

With a wave, he slipped into the crowd, maneuvering between a sea of people whose many conversations merged into a dull sigh. John strained to keep his father in sight, but quickly lost him in the confusion.

Surrounded by nervous chatter in an area containing hundreds, John felt, for the first time in his life, completely lost.

Eventually, the lone North Platte man found his way to a bench that was completely filled except for a spot on the end. Throwing his duffel down on the floor, John took a seat.

Looking at the scene surrounding him, John was simultaneously intrigued and sickened. The variety of people within the station was amazing. Individuals from all walks of life were mingling, their conversations peppered with words of Czech and German, both common ethnic groups in the area.

But as interesting as it was to watch the variety of people present in the train depot, John felt his heart get heavy each time he thought of his parents, and the decision he made to leave them.

"Did I do the right thing?," he wondered to himself.

Time trickled by slowly, but John's train eventually pulled into the station. He pulled himself aboard. Like the depot, the train was crowded and seats were hard to come by. After finding an empty place next to a young woman, he settled in for the two-and-a-half day trip that would take John first to Chicago, and then New York City.

At first, there was no conversation. The situations newness caused John's reserved nature to be magnified. But eventually boredom set in and he began visiting with the woman, who he guessed was three or four years older than himself.

John learned she had come to Lincoln from the Chicago area to visit her husband. The Air Force man was stationed in Nebraska, and she came to see him before being transferred. Although his destination was unknown, she guessed he would end up being stationed overseas.

The woman was apprehensive over the separation from her husband. They were newlyweds, really, married just under a year. But she realized her situation was not unique. Many others were going through the same thing. Her feelings were small, forgotten casualties in an effort that involved so many.

John relayed information about his home town, describing himself as a recent high school graduate whose first assignment in the Navy was "the big apple." By his own admission, he was as green as grass.

That night, sleep escaped John. Resting his head against the hard, uncomfortable coach seat, the car gently rocked from side to side. Mile after endless mile was counted out by the rail's rhythm—a clacking chant swallowed by nights restless embrace.

After what seemed like an eternity, light touched the eastern sky. After a brief stop in Chicago, the train headed eastward. Nine grueling hours later, the train pulled into Grand Central Station.

He was once again overwhelmed. Viewing his surroundings, John suddenly felt foolish at the awe he experienced in Omaha. Here, many more people milled about in much closer quarters. The heavy traffic and noise was overwhelming. Everyone seemed to be in a hurry and preoccupied with their own affairs. It was in sharp contrast to sleepy, peaceful North Platte, where a neighbors kindness was so easily taken for granted.

He was relieved to catch sight of an old family friend and distant relative who came to meet him. A long-time resident of New York City, the man was an advertising executive named Ted Hudson. Ted took John to a local restaurant near the train station where they had a good conversation about mutual acquaintances back home.

After dinner, Ted wrote down his phone number, some directions, and put John on the subway which took him to the battery. There, he caught a ferry boat to Staten Island and the training camp known as Manhattan Beach.

On the brief boat ride, John contemplated all he'd seen and heard during the last few days. It was all overwhelming. Yet, it was a time when the unsettling of peoples lives were so common, it was almost taken for granted.

12

After arriving at Manhattan Beach, military personnel directed him to a bunk house where he was to put his belongings. Then, the process of transforming from a civilian into a military man began.

For the next 90 days, emphasis was placed on learning to take orders unquestioningly and immediately. John was given a physical exam, shots, and issued Navy dress. It was there that young men were exposed to the duties of the service. It was there that ones life became that of the Navy.

John adjusted well to basic training. He arrived in good physical shape. Several years of putting up hay, fixing fence, and wrestling with calves had kept him toned while others struggled with the many physical challenges presented.

But the emotional aspect of what was happening was not so easy for John to accept. At times, the loneliness was overwhelming. As one of only two recruits from the Midwest, the rancher's son was a minority. Few at the training camp had any idea what it was like to grow up in Nebraska. Many didn't even know or care where Nebraska was. John was dumbfounded when a native New York recruit asked if people in Nebraska were still having problems with the Indians.

Still, he was more prepared to deal with military life than some who were there. But adjustment was a requirement and the playing field was leveled by the fact all were there for the same reason.

Therefore, John kept to himself, sharing little with those who surrounded him.

When 90 days were up, John was on the move once again. His company was sent to Ellis Island to join about 3,000 others also awaiting assignment.

A call for volunteers was sent out to anyone who preferred a certain branch of duty. Making a snap decision, John stepped forward to be assigned to sea duty. Doing so, his father's voice, advising him not to volunteer for anything, rang out in his mind.

Eventually, the entire group was dispersed to their respective destinations. Some went to shore duty, some to school if they were lucky and qualified. Within a short time, John found himself on a destroyer escort. It would be his home for the better part of two-and-a-half years.

***

Sara didn't think planning an evening of entertainment for servicemen would be to her liking. But to her surprise, it turned out to be right up her alley.

Of course, it had been her mother's idea. Organizing an evening for the entertainment of stateside soldiers was intended to be a grand display of support by the Hidden Valley social circle. Putting Sara in charge was designed to acquaint her with other social climbers dutifully supporting "their" home-town boys.

Sara knew the motives behind organizing the event were somewhat suspect, and initially resisted. But she'd put together several gatherings of a lesser sort at school with great success. And in this vacant time after high school graduation, the event was a welcome diversion.

Laura Manute, a classmate and friend, stood with Sara in a ballroom reserved for the event. Examining the sites circular, dome-shaped interior, the two discussed plans for the planned gala.

"Do you really think there will be enough seating in here?" Laura asked, rubbing her chin nervously.

"Well, if there isn't, we'll just have to bring in more chairs," Sara said as a sly look came over her face. "Or we could just have pesky Mrs. Butsky give up a few of the chairs she reserved. I don't really think the servicemen coming tomorrow night will need 30 chaperones looking over their shoulders."

"Well, maybe Mrs. Butsky just wants to fill her dance card for the night. It would be the first time in awhile for her, you know," Laura said, her round, freckled face lit with laughter.

"How true." Sara said, also chuckling lightly. "We should have invited her to graduation. I'm sure she would have kept things in line. Or at least crabby Principal Williams. He could use a little shaping up!"

The two girls erupted in laughter, delighting in the shared memory of their recent graduation ceremony.

It was an event Sara would remember fondly. Her parents took her into New York City to purchase a dress for the event.

Sara loved visiting the city. Smells of delicious, exotic foods mixed with heated fumes from passing cars. The hustle and bustle of people in every shape, size and color intrigued the girl of means. On the sidewalk, she enjoyed walking past small groups of French, Italian and Bohemian natives speaking in their native tongues. Sara would often find her feet slowing as she listened to the distinctive chatter of groups gathered at open cafes and beside gritty magazine stands.

Their voices were so mysterious, bantering back and forth. How nice it would be, Sara thought, to be included in such an intimate little group. To share in a joke and feel the kinsmanship of roots strong, yet invisible.

At night, stars overhead competed with twinkling red tail lights and marquees ablaze in light. Opera and symphony co-existed with the muted whine of jazz.

Sara and her parents spent the weekend enjoying the sights and sauntering easily between exclusive boutiques. The would-be graduate finally settled on a shimmering, floor-length satin gown. A pair of light gray pumps—exactly the same shade as her dress, later clipped elegantly as she walked across the stage to receive her diploma.

At a formal dance following the graduation, both singles and couples arrived in shiny chauffeured limousines. Young tuxedoed men swept partners in wide-flowing skirts across a glossy dance floor. Celebrating their emancipation from youth, the party lasted well into the night. As the clock chimed midnight, twilight fell on the graduates youth and brought in the dawn of adulthood.

Sara found the whole thing enchanting, dancing with almost every boy and exchanging laughter mixed with tearful farewells with her many girl friends. Although vaguely aware of the evenings excess, Sara realized the graduation party was a time-honored tradition. While designed for the graduates pleasure, everyone there knew the evening also carried a silent, underlying message. Because much was given to the graduates, much was expected in return. And while some would take advantage of the many opportunities offered them, others would not.

Still under the spell of that evening just days ago, Sara and Laura used the soldiers benefit as a crutch to bridge the now-empty gap in their lives.

With her eye on some high ceiling beams suitable for hanging decorations, Laura spoke more slowly. "So, Sara, what will you be doing for the next couple of months?"

"Oh, I don't know. I heard the college is offering a few summer classes. Thought I might enroll and get a head start on things. And daddy said some filing and typing jobs are waiting for me at his office. A girl I met at the library, Gretta McCloud, also invited me to a church picnic next week. That should be nice."

"Doesn't Gretta McCloud's dad work at my dad's factory?" Laura asked, eyes opened in surprise.

Sara knew well her mother's opinion of striking up relationships with those less affluent. It had caused a good deal of heated conversations between the two. Yet, Sara remained unimpressed with her mothers view.

Sara answered lightly.

"Why yes, I think so. I guess I didn't really think to ask."

"A church picnic inside the city? I'm sure your mom will love that!"

Crossing her arms, Sara looked at Laura evenly. "Well, maybe I'll just have to take mother with me. She might like to see how the other half lives!"

"Oh, I've met your mother. That isn't very likely," Laura said, shaking her head and laughing.

"So what do you think? Red balloons, or blue?," Sara said, intentionally changing the subject.

***

After a few weeks, life aboard the destroyer became routine. John's Navy career began as a Seaman, Second Class. But he quickly left his job as a deck hand and was promoted to a Radar man, Third Class. He was entrusted with manning radar equipment and operating a sound machine designed to detect underwater activity.

As the ship set off across the Atlantic, a social order developed among the ships crew. A large number of John's mates were from the East coast. Several were Italian, New York natives who had never ventured out of the city. The men formed their own close knit clique, from which a North Platte boy was easily excluded.

Of the 130 aboard, John guessed that only about five or six were from the Midwest. These young men gravitated toward each other, forming a tight knit group within the ships confines.

Regardless of the ethnic background or home town, the diverse group quartered together within the ships narrow confines did share one commonality. Almost all were draftees, forced to embrace a common goal. Everyone looked forward to the war coming to an end. And almost all anticipated returning to the lives they knew before war became a reality in their lives.

One day flowed into the next as the destroyer tirelessly cut it's way across the Atlantic. The ship primarily accompanied merchant ships carrying war materials to allies. For the most part things went along smoothly. Occasionally the ship went on high alert when German submarines were detected in allied waters. Each time the threat passed, John and his shipmates breathed a sigh of relief.

John never took to the sea. Often, he would gaze down at the water, imagining the endless ocean as sandhills grass blowing across the prairie. He struggled with the question of whether he should remain in the service after the war was over, or return home. But in time he came to realize a true sailor prefers the sea, while a cowboy prefers the land.

On occasion, the monotony of ship life was broken by a stop at New York Harbor. When there, many on board were able to go home for visits with family and friends. Those from the Midwest seldom got this luxury. During these times, John made an effort to see the sights, or headed for a service canteen for some entertainment.

But as John's ship slid into dock on May 7, 1945, crew members were greeted with surprising news. Germany had surrendered, and the knowledge spread like wildfire throughout the ship.

John watched as thousands and thousands of people poured into Manhattan's Times Square. A huge celebration that lasted two days ensued. It was a much-anticipated and hard-won victory.

As John awaited word about his Navy status, he was assigned to a harbor patrol boat. Personnel was steadily dispersed. Many used the opportunity to review their lives. A large number of John's comrades went home to plan their next move in life. Some went on to school. Others decided to try their hand at life in a different part of the country.

Boarding the same train he arrived on months earlier, John bid farewell to New York, looking homeward with anticipation. The long journey gave him plenty of time to think. Inevitably, his mind turned to thoughts of the ranch and the life he knew there.

Closing his eyes, he envisioned the tidy white ranch house he called home for so many years. After his experiences in New York and at sea, John longed for wide-open spaces and the sight of friendly, familiar faces. As the train lumbered into Omaha, a decision became clear to the North Platte native who so recently bid farewell to boyhood. He would go home, and there he would stay.

As the train slid into Omaha's station, John eagerly peered out the window for a glimpse of his parents. Standing on the platform, the two were a joy to behold. Yet, it was obvious something was different.

Ed was unusually thin and his face held an alarming ashen color. Greeting them both warmly with hugs, his dear mother also appeared worn and more fragile than John had ever known her to be.

Escaping the stations frenzy, the trio ambled towards a nearby coffee house. There, Ed and Helen filled John in. A heart attack had seized Ed just two months before, throwing the family ranch into turmoil. For a time, the frantic parents were considering asking the military for a hardship discharge.

But good neighbors had pitched in to help. The Olson's shook their heads as they recounted the kindness and generosity friends had shown throughout their difficulties.

As Ed spoke, his son examined his weary face and work-worn hands. He was saddened that the man he loved and grew up admiring was failing. John had watched as his father threw bales and wrestled calves with what appeared the strength of three men. A sense of protectiveness formed in John's breast as he realized his parents were gracefully sliding into the autumn of their lives just as summer dawned on his.

Gathering himself up, John spoke with a sense of newfound maturity and strength.

"Don't worry, mom and dad. Things will be different now that I'm here to stay."

As they walked to the car, Ed threw John the keys. Sliding into the drivers seat, the car headed westward. Omaha and the past faded into the distance. The trio sensed something new between them as they sailed down the highway. John was home, and the time to begin anew was at hand.

Pulling onto the long, dusty driveway leading to their house, John was surprised to see friends and neighbors gathered to greet him. Hugs and handshakes were dotted with laughter and cheerful banter as the group settled in to enjoy a Nebraska-style steak feed.

Seated at a picnic table and downing an icy glass of lemonade, John reflected on those around him. How good it was to get out of the sailor suit and back into cowboy boots and jeans. Home at last!

***

"Studying and tests, tests and books. I have had just about enough," Sara thought to herself.

Carrying an arm-load of books, Sara trudged across campus to the library. It was time for finals, and she had just finished taking her last exam. After turning in a couple term papers, she would be ready for a much deserved break.

It had been almost two years since Sara first set foot on the Sandhurst college campus. Thanks to taking a few extra classes each semester and during the summer, she was just a few credit hours shy of being a senior.

Much had been happening in Sara's life. Following a somewhat anxious post-high school summer, she had arrived on campus. Moving into a dorm was an eye-opening experience for the only child of a wealthy Manhattan couple. Hemmed in by parents and young adults burdened by the weight of suitcases, the whole building had appeared chaotic.

But Sara adjusted quickly. Pledging to a sorority, she'd had the opportunity to meet many people on campus during the next several months. And amazingly, she'd been able to forge the kind of friendships that seemed out of reach while at her exclusive high school. At college, she was able to meet people from all walks of life. And while many of these people were not what her mother would have called "appropriate," Sara found herself enjoying their company immensely.

As she thought about it, Sara came to realize that it was the diversity of viewpoints that was most intriguing. Although at the time it wasn't apparent, most of the people she grew up with were alike. They knew the same people, vacationed at the same places, even shopped the same stores.

College, though, brought people of more varied backgrounds together. True, most of them were still middle to upper class, but Sara's peers came from throughout the country. It was refreshing to talk about her life with new people. And the experiences others shared were intriguing to such an inexperienced young woman.

The sacrifices these people made to attend college also amazed Sara. A few had part-time jobs to help pay their way. Sara, on the other hand, had always left the financial obligations and concerns to her father, never giving them any thought.

While home was only about a two-hour drive from college, Sara gradually returned there less and less. During breaks, the tension between she and her mother seemed to become increasingly difficult to deal with.

In a way, Sara knew it was her own fault. Many times, she knew her mother would be exasperated by things she said even before they came out her her mouth. But Sara felt as though school had opened up a new world to her. And even though her mother might object, the young woman wanted her parents to know about the changes taking place within her.

Without realizing it, Sara was letting her parents know where she was in her life. By sharing her thoughts unguardedly, Sara was unconsciously seeking approval. And on the way to that understanding, perhaps Agnes would grow to understand her daughter. A daughter she saw so differently in her mind.

Chapter 3

Western Nebraska was not a place for the weak-hearted.

In its infancy, it was comprised of the hardiest adventurers—solid, steadfast individuals who firmly believed hard work would yield a better life. The area was home to the buffalo and Indians, considered an outpost of the American frontier.

As the Union Pacific railroad moved westward, homesteaders whose livelihood was farming and ranching, followed. In the end, only the strongest remained. The rest returned to the east, or pushed westward in search of opportunity.

John's roots were firmly embedded in that tradition—a way of life that began with his grandparents. He learned early on what it meant to put in a hard days work. Battling burning summer heat and bitterly cold winters was the life of a prairie settler—the life of a survivor.

As the days following John's arrival home melted into weeks, he found comfort in that tradition. Looking out at the rolling hills that seemed to meet the horizon, his thoughts often drifted to those who had come before him. What spell, he wondered, did this land cast over his ancestors? What lure did it have to hold them despite it's many cruelties?

John didn't know the answers. But he did know that in coming home, the gently-flowing land was a comfort. Cattle complacently grazing in green pastures, calling out in low, comforting melody, brought him joy. Within it's quiet beauty, a peace came over him which had flitted away like a delicate, lone milkweed seed caught up by an incessant north wind. Here, his heart was light again—the sea's burden finally lifted.

Doing his chores, John couldn't help but see his world in a different light. A life illuminated by the tedious glare military service had provided. Activities that once seemed mundane were now a privilege to be reveled in. Life's routine blanketed John, comforting his memory from the stress it had known while at sea.

Venturing into town, he renewed old friendships and resumed his life. Saturday nights brought trips to the tavern, a few beers and a few hardy laughs.

Occasionally, John would find himself on a date. But, his experiences during the war had drained John emotionally, and he happily returned to the solitary life he chose.

***

Months passed, and the Olson's ranch flourished. Thanks to John's management, good weather, and hard work luck smiled on the trio. As the cattle herd increased in size, John and his father began to realize they needed help. After placing an ad in the local newspaper, all they could do was wait.

A few days later, John and his parents were on their porch. Their conversation stopped as an old blue pickup turned into their driveway. Dust billowed from behind the truck, and as it drew nearer John noticed it was dented and rusted in several spots. It drew to a stop with brakes squeaking. The door flew open and a tall, thin man who looked about 45 emerged.

As the visitor sauntered to the porch, Helen covered her mouth to hide her amusement. Although his clothes appeared well kept and clean, his large 10-gallon hat sported two huge dents that looked as though it had been run over by a car. At first glance, it appeared as if their visitor was wearing a lopsided dunce cap.

The faint shadow of a graying beard covered his face. Deep lines foretold of days spent squinting beneath a bright sun. Light red veins formed a spider web across his cheeks. Sharp blue eyes peered out curiously beneath salt-and-pepper brows that crept across his face like restless caterpillars.

The man spoke slowly, using a bent, calloused finger to tip his hat brim.

"Howdy ma'am. Sirs. I'm here in answer to your ad-verse-ment for a hired hand."

Working his lips, the stranger turned his head to the side and spat out a brown arch of chew that landed with a splat a few feet away.

"Name's Zeke Clarkson. Pleased to make your acquaintance." As he extended his hand, first Ed, then John reached out to return the greeting. Glancing past the newcomer to his truck, Ed squinted to make out the license plate.

"Looks like your a little ways from home."

"Well, yes sir. You see, I'm com'in in from Colorada territory. Seems Jim Bray, the man I've been work'in for these past four years, is done tired of the business. He's fix'in to retire, 'an tol me I jus' as well head out and look for another job. Was just pass'in through when I picked up a paper and saw your ad." Reaching into a shirt pocket, he pulled out a sheet of paper. "Even got me a letter 'o recommendation from Mr. Bray. Says anybody who wonts can give him a call any time and he'd be happy to vouch fer me."

John stepped forward to examine the paper.

"So you've worked cattle before. What else can you do?," John asked.

"Well, thes'in last few years I've done a good deal of fence fix'in. Mr. Bray got into them wild horses, too, so I done me some break'in. Oh, let me tell you—that's the life. Rid'in a wild one, and not even a rodeo crowd to watch ya!"

Zeke's face erupted into a grin exposing an uneven row of brown teeth. Ed smiled, nodding in understanding.

"Well, we don't get much of that out here. Stick mostly with the cattle."

"Then I'm your man," Zeke said, rubbing his bristled chin lightly. "I bin around cattle all my life. Grew up on a ranch near the border. But the family's all gone now. Just the old cow poke you see here left."

"Looks like your old employer thought highly of you," John said, briefly shaking the letter Zeke handed him.

"Yessir. He did indeed right that of his own free will. Didn't even have to get my gun out," Zeke said, the lines on his face flowering into laughter.

Stepping forward, John spoke. "Tell you what. We'll give it a try and see how it works out. You can put your things in the bunk house over to the east of the house. You'll be eating with the family. My mother, Helen, will do the cooking."

"Oh, I jus can't thank you enough. I can promise you—you won't be sorry," Zeke said, a grateful smile tickling his lips.

"You won't be sorry."

In the days to come, Zeke did prove to be an outstanding ranch hand. When working with cattle, he seemed to instinctively know what the animals were thinking. Even ornery, wild calves fresh off the prairie and scared to death of humans found Zeke an equal match. Bent on escaping during roundups, they would dart wildly, intent on retaking freedom.

But Zeke would doggedly follow such runaways, patiently coaxing his horse left, right, then left again. Exhausted, the stubborn calves would eventually submit, opting to join the herd rather than continue fighting.

Still, Zeke was not without a few warts. The Olsons quickly learned their hired hand liked to drink. On Saturday nights he would head for the local tavern, downing several before staggering home.

Late one Saturday, the Olsons got a call from the sheriff's office. Zeke was being held in county jail overnight. Apparently, he was overcome by alcohol and began making a fool of himself downtown. Sunday morning John drove into the city and brought him back to the ranch. He was hung over all day Sunday. But Monday morning he was back on the job as good as ever.

Gradually, he became like a member of the family. As time went on, the four built a comfortable rapport. Even Helen, who had a marked dislike for Zeke's chewing habit, made a point of keeping an empty coffee can close by the dinner table.

"I'd rather see him spit tobacco juice in the can, than watch him swallow it," she grudgingly admitted.

***

The final year of Sara's college began slipping by. Walking across campus she noticed that summer's green exuberance had slowly disappeared. Yellow, orange and red leaves dressed the trees and rained down with each passing breeze.

Sara was stirred by the change in seasons. It brought out a faint sense of optimism—a feeling that had become quite infrequent. As Sara's final fall semester at college began, a sense of anxiety about what lay ahead teased her mind. True, the college experience had broadened her base of knowledge. Her job possibilities, at least, were promising. And overall, college life had agreed with the indulged Hidden Valley native. Her grades had continued to be good, and there was no reason to believe this final year would be any different.

As she walked across campus, a cool northern breeze numbed Sara's cheeks and nose. Tucking gloved hands into the pockets of a smart-looking gray and white plaid coat, her thoughts drifted into the past.

Three years of living away from her parents had agreed with Sara. She felt a sense of release in being allowed to follow pursue her own interests and choose her own friends. Without the burden of financial worries, she was able to enjoy almost all the social activities her school had to offer.

Sara stopped for a minute and gazed up at campus buildings that reached up to the cloudless blue sky. All around her, students scampered about. Clutching their coat collars with one hand, and a stack of books in the other, everyone seemed to be on urgent business. Papers were due, impending tests were just around the corner. And it seemed as though there was never enough time to do it all.

The thought of all these people taking themselves so seriously amused Sara. "What would happen if they all just stopped," she wondered to herself. A smile touched her lips as she imagined shocked professors with no term papers to correct—nobody to receive their detailed lectures.

Sara shook her head as if to clear it. "How ridiculous. After all, we are here to learn," she berated herself angrily.

It wasn't the first time Sara had caught herself daydreaming and imagining an escape from the constant demands college imposed. Yet, her negative feelings persisted. She had earned good grades, made good friends. But the girl raised in the posh Hidden Valley neighborhood realized true happiness was not yet hers. Something was missing from her life.

Exactly what was missing, however, remained elusive. It was a knowledge just beyond her reach—a truth richly adorned in a lustrous golden challis.

But the reward that was to be hers remained enshrouded behind a thin veil of fog. If she closed her eyes, Sara could almost imagine it in the distance. But just as she felt understanding was near, yet another curtain—this one thick and impenetrable— swooped down heavily, blanketing it's secret determinedly.

Straining in vein, Sara knew the trophy and the rich reward it held would not yet be hers. The weight it held over her heart would remain oppressive. Her ability to understand her feelings slinked into the shadows, unwilling to be coaxed out until the comforting voice of time called out, assuring a safe approach.

Frustrated by her inability to understand the heaviness in her heart, Sara shuffled along, watching as a whirlwind spun magical brews of leaves and dust in the air.

Perhaps it's better not to dwell, Sara thought. After all, what good would it do? And she had much to look forward to as graduation grew closer. Finding a job wouldn't be a problem.She was encouraged by the interest some had already shown in hiring her. True, some of her father's acquaintances offered her positions in the field of business. But she had also sent some inquiries to schools in the area. Some had expressed the desire to interview her for teaching positions after graduation. One prestigious school had even tentatively offered her a job.

Still, that empty, heavy feeling persisted. It was something she carried with her throughout the day. At times, her confusion was almost too much to bear, and she would begin to cry. As she wiped her dampened eyes, Sara sometimes felt better. But the release was short-lived, building up ever so slowly as tests and lectures bumped against sophisticated sorority social events. Then she would find herself alone once again in a crowd. An unwilling participant in an ongoing theater melodrama, where the heroes and heroines were indifferent to their roles and the plot lacked a clear direction.

"Maybe dad will know what to do," she concluded. By now, Sara had reached the doorway of the on-campus student union. The warm air rushed to meet her, pinching her winter-kissed cheeks. Students were gathered around tables, some studying, some exchanging the latest stories. The building always had the smell of fresh bakery from a small diner near the buildings entrance. The warmth, smells and thoughts of speaking to her father seemed to mingle, bolstering Sara's drooping spirits.

"Yes, dad will know what to do," she said, a small bounce returning to her step.

Sitting across from her father three weeks later, Sara did approach him with her concerns. They were seated together in a cozy parlor, the fireplace ablaze. Agnes was out for the evening, and Joe was seated in a plush easy chair, flipping through the evening paper. The room's warm glow lulled Sara into dreamy comfort. During much of the week she had been home, the Morris' had been on a continuous social whirl. Holiday parties were in full swing in Hidden Valley. Sara touched base with several of her old high school friends.

As she sat by her father, the same feeling of apprehension that followed her through the hallways of Sandhurst college began to surface once again. Cautiously, Sara to speak.

"Dad, I've been thinking a lot during the past few months. I don't know. Things should be looking up, but I just feel lost.."

Joe lowered his arms, allowing his newspaper to fall to his lap. He was surprised by his daughter's somber tone. Since her return home, she had appeared happy—even boisterous at times. As he looked at the young woman before him, however, he quickly realized his error in judgment. This was the real Sara, the thoughtful daughter he knew well. The personality she brought home from college was someone quite different. A personality created to protect the daughter who lay beneath.

"Yes," Joe said slowly, tossing the newspaper to the ground, "Now that you mention it, I did notice something was troubling you. Is it your grades? Someone giving you a hard time at school?"

"Oh no-no. Nothing like that," Sara assured him. "It's just that. I don't know. I can't really put my finger on it. I guess I just don't know where I'm going from here. I don't really know what I should be looking for in life."

Joe nodded his head in understanding. The years dissolved as he recalled his own struggle to find direction so many years ago.

"Yes, I believe that's something we must all go through. And unfortunately, there is no right answer. It is up to you to find your way and follow a path that suits you."

Although she didn't think it was possible, Sara's heart plunged even further down. In talking to her father, she had hoped he would provide some answers—a tried and true map that would help her make some sense of her life. Instead, she felt herself slipping further and further downward, her frantic cries for some sense of direction in her life fluttering away.

"But that's just it, dad. I'm afraid I will choose the wrong path. And then what? I'll be stuck in a job or place or with people I won't be happy with."

Joe's heart ached for his daughter, whose indecision was obviously wearing away at her. But he refused to send her in the direction of his choosing.

"Sara, I understand. But this is something you'll have to figure out on your own. And you will figure it out. You will know when the decision is right. All you can do now is take it one day at a time."

The two sat silently, both staring into the fire. One torn by a fear of the unknown, and the other, saddened by the struggle. Each reflected on the situation from different perspectives sketched out by life's wavering hand.

"You know, school has been keeping you so busy, and Lord knows your mother could have you at a different social event every day. Maybe it would help if you would get some distance from both for awhile. You know, aunt and uncle Bernoulli are always inviting you over. Maybe you should take them up on it during the next break," Joe said.

Sara thought the idea over. Yes, it was true. She needed some time to get away. She had always liked her father's sister, Mary, and her husband, Ted, and had many fond memories of times she spent with them in their Denver home. They always seemed so down-to-earth, yet always ready to have some fun. The last time Sara visited about five years ago, their four children were all still at home. While their mountain-side residence was large, Sara was struck by the hustle and bustle of activity in the household. Everyone had someplace to go and something to do.

It all made Sara feel energized—something she badly needed. It would be nice to see them all again. Because it would be Christmas break, some of the older Bernoulli siblings would be visiting. Her favorite, Kim, now a college sophomore, would also be home.

Sara always liked to hear about Kim's many adventures. When still living at home, she would occasionally offer ski lessons at a local resort. She would go on for hours, talking about interesting people and experiences on the slopes. It was a relationship Sara was grateful to have and looked forward to continuing.

After vacation, Sara knew she would resume classes and begin an internship at a nearby elementary school. As the new year of 1949 dawned, she would begin sending out applications. By the time graduation day approached, Sara felt sure a job opportunity would be waiting.

Yes, now would be her only chance to get away and make sense of things.

"All right," she said, smiling. "Anything is worth a try."

***

It was December 24, 1948, and everything at the Olson ranch appeared to lie in wait of the upcoming Christmas holiday. A large cedar tree had been hauled in from the pasture and set up in the families living room. Outside, the tree had appeared to be small. But in order to fit it into a corner spot, it was necessary to rearrange the furniture and even take one easy chair out of the room entirely. The cedars sprawling branches, and rich, green smell reached out.

To give the tree a snow-topped appearance, Mrs. Olson had whipped up a thick, frothy broth of soap and smeared it generously over the branches. Delicate glass bells and ornamental globes in shades of red and green danced in the evening light.

Even the animals housed in the barn outside appeared to lay in wait of the upcoming holiday. As was the tradition at the Olson's, all the animals outside got a larger-than-normal portion of feed. With full bellies the cattle lounged lazily atop a bedding of straw, contentedly chewing their cuds.

As usual, Mrs. Olson had planned a huge Christmas meal, complete with a plump turkey and steaming pumpkin pie. This year the family felt particularly grateful. The cattle herd had done well, and few animals were lost because of sickness or bad weather. Zeke continued to be a great help, which kept Ed in good health and high spirits.

And of course, John had not forgotten his war-time experiences. Compared to his time spent at sea, Christmas time in North Platte was heaven on earth.

In the past few years, a sense of optimism and self-assuredness had grown within him. John had come to realize his concerns about becoming a rancher had been unfounded. Cattle prices had continued to hold up well and resulted in a profitable calf crop. Ample fall rains meant an abundant hay crop.

John was doing very well for himself. In fact, he had recently began entertaining the idea of expanding his ranch operation. But his father, a graduate from the school of hard knocks, cautioned his son. Ed had seen farmers and ranchers lose everything from drought or poor prices. Bankers, once so willing to extend loans, could suddenly have a change of heart, cutting off credit and ending a ranchers livelihood with just a few stokes of a pen. He cautioned his son against expanding too rapidly. John had taken his father's words to heart, and so far held off from any major decisions.

But deep down, John knew ranching was the life for him. It was here that he was happy. He loved working with the cattle, hearing their soft lowing calls blend with birds song and the winds gentle whisper. Here, he could be his own boss, free to enjoy fraternizing with good neighbors, or isolate himself in solitudes quiet serenity.

Deep down, he hoped to find someone who would share his appreciation for the life he loved. Someone who could appreciate nature's divine secrets and understand the joy of experiencing God's many silent but profound gifts.

Christmas Eve night was clear and cold as the Olson's made their way to midnight services. The car tires crunched through a foot of hardened snow, following grooves etched in the driveway earlier. So far, two storms had hit the area, but had done little to hinder daily activities.

As they drove to the church a bright, full moon cast a glow over the countryside. Snow on barren corn fields and within roadside ditches glistened like diamonds sprinkled generously from the heavens.

The Lutheran church stood as it had for decades, welcoming all to enter. It's straight, white clapboard exterior spoke of strength and age. The surrounding valley seemed to embrace the place of worship, providing a haven from what lay beyond.

As John pulled into a parking place, he was taken by the evening's enchantment. Men and women, some with children in tow, some arm in arm, trotted into the church, racing from winter's chill. They reminded John of cumbersome winter fairies returning from a night of merrymaking.

Walking to the churches doors, his breath wafted upwards, a veil drifting away effortlessly to reveal his soul. It was a time for miracles, and stepping into the church's quiet stillness, John sensed that something was about to change.

Chapter 4

For Sara, it had been a long two months.

After returning from Christmas break, the grueling school routine had continued. She tried to keep herself distracted by throwing herself into social activities. But the anxiety of her upcoming graduation was never far from her mind. The questions of her unresolved future plans dangled, just out of reach.

Thank goodness she had the upcoming break to look forward to. The way had been cleared for her Colorado visit with relatives. As she boarded a train destined for the country's heart, she prepared to leave behind her east-coast mentality.

While there, she hoped to find some sense of peace in what could be a tumultuous time following graduation. She was overwhelmed by the need to find some meaning in her life — a sense of urgency prompting her to choose the right path.

Sara was confident her aunt and uncle could help her. With so many children of their own, surely they had faced similar struggles. And their honest, down to earth attitude about life was always a comfort to Sara. In the world she grew up in, it seemed so easy to get lost in an unending series of events and the ongoing saga of other's lives.

Mary and Ted had a way of simplifying things. They knew how to strip off the confection to see things for what they really were. It wasn't that they were harsh people. If anything, they were much more kind and considerate than most of the people Sara knew. But not being subjected to the petty ramblings and social pecking order common in the Olson's social circle allowed them to have a more honest perspective. And it was that honest perspective that Sara was counting on to get her through this difficult time.

The train rumbled on for two days, giving Sara plenty of time to reflect. She spent the time staring at the countryside, watching the landscape flit by. The seat adjacent to her was occupied by two different people during the journey. Sara took it upon herself to strike up a conversation with each of them, anxious to hear their stories and temporarily abandon her own concerns.

One, an elderly man from Maine, was on his way to Iowa to visit his son. The two hadn't seen each other for quite some time, and the man was anxious to become reacquainted with his grandchildren.

The man was a World War I veteran. A few hours into the journey, he began to share bits and pieces of information about his life — a wife who recently passed away, a house that was no longer a home without her. And then, his mind turned to the past, and a youth lost to the ravages of war.

His eyes clouded over as he related stories of his wartime travels. In a lilting Irish accent , he spoke of long, terrifying nights spent in far away European lands. Places where softly rolling land was transformed into bloody battlefields.

Through it all, Sara listened attentively, and the elderly man warmed to the attention she offered. Many were tired of his stories, or too busy and distracted to care. But for the young Hidden Valley girl, his ramblings were a revelation — a look at something new that she had never before considered. She had never actually talked to someone who had been in active battle. War had always been something far away that was serious, but didn't really have any bearing on day to day activities. But the elderly man sitting beside her was a key to a collective history she knew nothing about. He simultaneously opened a door to that in the human spirit that is at once mystifying and terrifying.

Encouraged by her interest, the man continued on with a sense of urgency. His voice mused on mile after mile, a sense of urgency to retell his stories before time ran out. He revived tales of friends and comrades he knew along the way, and pondered the irony fate played in putting them together as it did.

In the midst of their visit, Sara considered the many young men who had just returned from World War II. Few were willing to discuss their experiences. Once they got back to the families and lives they left behind, it seemed as if present-day concerns squeezed unpleasant memories from their mind.

But in talking to the old man, Sara realized that while old wounds may be forgotten by the mind, the heart continues to embrace it's losses. Like a miser counts and recounts coins until the faces are worn smooth, the heart returns, time and again, to revisit it's pain.

By the time the old veteran bid her farewell, Sara felt as though they were old friends who had shared something real. She watched from her window as a tall, dark-haired man, undoubtedly the veteran's son, greeted him with a warm hug. And as the train pulled out of the station, she felt herself slipping into the old gentleman's past, just like so many others in his life had.

A young girl, about 12 years of age, took the old man's spot. She worked the handle of her satchel nervously. It wasn't long before Sara befriended the girl, who it turned out was on her first train ride. Destined for Nebraska, she was going to spend time with her grandparents while her parents grappled with some financial difficulties. Three of her other siblings had already been sent away to live with aunts and uncles in other parts of the country. As the oldest, she was the last to go.

The young girl didn't know what the future would hold, or even if the day her family reunited would ever take place. The young girl began to cry as she admitted her situations uncertainty. And Sara's efforts to comfort her sounded hollow to her ears.

"Who am I to tell her it's going to get better?," Sara asked herself. Her own future, at times, seemed as unsettled as the young girls. But Sara knew her situation was considerable different. And so, she offered what condolences she could.

After the girl got off the train, the seat next to Sara remained vacant. As the passenger train swayed from side to side, she had several hours to think about the two fellow travelers she came to know. They were both so different, separated by decades of time. Yet both were in search of something. To Sara, it appeared as though they were reaching out, desperately flailing to find that thread which links all humanity. To find someone to listen, to care, to love.

The lights of Denver came into view, like a star constellation on the midnight blue horizon. Sara knew that while her journey by train would soon be ending, her journey in life was just about to begin.

As the train finally pulled to a stop, Sara arose. Her legs were stiff from being seated for so long, but she forced them to work as she clutched a railing for support. But she quickly forgot her ails when she caught sight of Mary and Ted, along with Kim waiting in the depot.

Giving them all a hug and kiss, Sara smiled broadly. "I'm so glad to see you," she kept saying over and over. "I'm so glad to be here."

***

Sara was to spend a week with the Bernoulli's in their mountainside home. It became clear from the start her visit would be an adventure. The area was covered by at least three feet of snow. In order to get to the Bernoulli home, which was located several miles from the station, the foursome jumped into a horse-drawn sleigh.

"Oh I know, it's plenty old fashioned," Ted said, "But it's a lot more reliable than a car right now. The icy roads are causing all kinds of cars to slide off the road into the ditch."

"Yes, we get tired of having to walk for help," Mary chimed in.

Sara was pleased to see Mary and Ted hadn't changed a bit since the last time she'd visited them. Ted was still his sturdy old self. Although it was hard to make out a face beneath his trademark coon-skin hat with ear flaps, his twinkling blue eyes and jovial smile were still evident. His slight plumpness wasn't camouflaged by the thick, down-filled coat he wore.

Mary, like Sara's father, was tall and thin. Small lines around her eyes and mouth told of a face accustomed to laughter. Sara always thought there was something regal about her aunt. Even now, bundled beneath layers of coats and blankets, she looked more like a queen setting out to visit important dignitaries rather than the wife of a trapper and store owner.

Kim snuggled underneath a blanket next to Sara. At once, the two were caught up in their old, familiar camaraderie.

"So, what brings you all the way out here?" Kim asked.

"Why, a train, of course," Sara bantered back playfully.

"Oh, you New York girls always have all the answers. Just wait until tomorrow. I can't wait to see how your skiing has come along."

"Oh! It hasn't!," Sara laughed, "I haven't been skiing since I was here last time!"

"Well, we need to bring you up to speed, silly. Maybe I can even help you run into some cute boys — or was that your plan?," Kim said, ribbing Sara lightly.

"You know me, all work and no play," Sara said, pretending to pout.

"Right. Yea. That's you all right."

The two kept up their chatter for the rest of the ride home, alternately exchanging information about their lives and slipping in a good humored bit of teasing.

When they arrived at the Bernoulli's snug cabin, Sara's face was stinging from the cold night air. A sweet, smoky smell drifted from the homes chimney and scented the surrounding woodland. She eagerly slipped from beneath the warm blanket covering her legs, and ran to find the warm hearth promised by the rich, delicious fragrance.

Once in the door, three of Sara's cousins crowded around to meet her. For several minutes, warm hugs and fleeting kisses were exchanged. Conversations were mingled into a frenzy of brief snippets. "What have you been up to's" mixed with "My, but you look wonderful." Eventually, Sara was whisked to a spot in front of the fireplace, where the flames appeared to reach out and swipe away the air's chill.

As the evening ebbed away and a new day weakly stepped in to take over, conversation continued. Two of Sara's cousins had also returned home earlier that day, and were still full of information to share about their lives at college. Finally, as the clock struck two, Ted slapped his knees and stood up.

"Well, it looks as though I'll have to call it a day. I've got an appointment to meet a group of hunters at daybreak, and that doesn't leave much time for sleep. Good night everyone, and see you tomorrow afternoon."

Ted's departure set off a domino effect in the room, and everyone began stretching and yawning. Sara followed Kim to her bedroom, and the place the two had shared so many childhood giggles and secrets.

Exhausted, the two fell into bed. Almost immediately, Kim's breath slowed to the deep, steady rhythm of sleep. But although she was exhausted from her journey, sleep did not greet Sara easily. For a time, she tossed and turned, listening to the murmur of voices down the hall. Eventually, they, too, ceased and were replaced with the gentle purrs and creaks of the wood side cabin.

The sights Sara saw during the past few days swirled around, playing an endless game of tag in her mind. She imagined herself back on the train, the steady sway and rhythmic clank of iron against iron enveloping her. Suddenly, she was back in her seat. The old World War I veteran and young, scared girl were seated together, facing Sara. The two talked, one with wisdom's voice, the other, youth's naive unrest. They spoke of their lives and fears, what came to pass and where the future might lead.

Sara was struck by how their differences seemed to disappear. Each needed a confidant, someone who could offer understanding as the unknown lurked dubiously. The elder drew strength from his counterparts youth. He was reminded of himself, so long ago, and the decisions he made that led him to the winter of his life. And she drew solace from his age, and the wisdom life had brought him.

Both were searching for that missing piece of the puzzle which would assure their survival, an assurance their efforts served a purpose. As the young girl reached out and gently patted the old man's hand, the vision blurred, calling Sara away.

During the next few days, Sara enjoyed becoming reacquainted with her relatives. She and Kim took long walks through the woods, catching up on their lives. Like Sara, Kim had found college life agreeable. Yet, she had none of Sara's ambivalence in discussing her future plans. Kim had a good head for business, and planned on getting an accounting degree. And Sara listened in interest as Kim discussed her romantic interest in a classmate.

As they sat on a snow-covered tree that had fallen in the woods, Sara couldn't help but question her cousin further.

"Well, Kim, just how serious are the two of you?," she asked, propping herself against the tree trunk.

"Oh, you know what they say, 'love at first sight.' I don't know. We've talked about the future some. He's a fun, interesting person. I guess I'll just have to wait and see.

They paused in quiet contemplation.

"So, are you telling me you haven't met anyone while at college?," Kim said, breaking the silence.

"Well, sure. I mean, I've been on dates with a lot of different guys while at college. But to be honest, I just haven't been very impressed. They're all kind of the same, you know? There's not one that stands out," Sara said, thinking of her many acquaintances.

"Well, if you'd met the right one, I'm sure you'd know it. Let's see, what is it... about three months until graduation? What are your plans?"

Sara paused for a moment, thrown by the question. Yes, she'd sent out applications and had a vague goal in mind. But the word plan suggested some method should be involved in her final decision-making. It led her to imagine a series of gradual steps designed to get her to a final goal, rather than making a single, drastic decision. As she turned the idea over in her mind, she suddenly realized that while her choices after graduation could set her course, it was not final. Her decision could be just the first of many that would lead to her ultimate goal—whatever that may be.

"Oh, I don't know. I guess I'll try to get into teaching. You know, just get a little experience. If that doesn't work out, I guess I'll go to plan B," Sara said, smiling at the simplicity of it all.

"Well, it's nice to have a back up plan. What is plan B, by the way?"

"If teaching doesn't work out, I guess it's off to the world of business. I've taken quite a few classes in management. Not a lady-like possibility according to my mother. She would just as soon I stay at home, marry some rich kid from down the block and start having children," Sara said.

"I did notice that was never one of your main goals," Kim said, laughing.

"Oh, and what gave it away," Sara said, joining her.

Later that evening, after the supper dishes had been cleared away, Kim went out to help her brothers gather firewood. Sara and Mary sat down beside the kitchen table, sipping mugs of piping-hot cider.

Mary looked thoughtfully at her niece. She had grown up so much in the last few years. But even though she was almost a college graduate, Mary sensed Sara was still very much the little girl she once knew.

"Sara, I'm so glad you came to visit us. And it's so nice you could come when the others were home, too."

"Oh, I was looking forward to it. I figured that after graduation things might become, well, more complicated."

"Yes, I'm sure you'll be busy. But you will be able to keep things into perspective."

"It would be the first time. It seems like I've been just hanging on these past few months."

"You mean, with all the studying?"

"Well, that, too. But mostly just worrying about what's going to happen after I graduate. I guess I'm a little scared."

"Well, you've got your feet firmly planted. It just takes time to get it all worked out."

"The thing is, I was never concerned like this before. When I graduated from high school, I knew the next step would be college. But now..."

"But now, you're on new ground. That's because it's time for you to choose your own direction. It's just another step to growing up. You'll do fine. Just relax and think things through. Sometimes, its easier to work your way backwards. Think about what you'd like to tell your grandchildren when you're an old lady in a rocking chair."

Sara smiled, the vision of her as a grandmother formed clearly in her mind.

"That one, aunt Mary, I'll have to take more slowly."

"And that, child, is the way it should be."

37

Before she knew it, Sara's Colorado stay came to an end. She was to leave on a Friday morning. The Bernoulli's opened their garage door, the seldom-used hinges squeaking in protest, and coaxed their four-door Chrysler into reverse. Only Mary and Ted accompanied Sara to the train. Kim and her two brothers were heading off later in the day, and were in the middle of a packing frenzy as Sara left. With a few brief kisses and hugs, Sara waved goodbye and headed out the door. She settled into the car's foamy green interior and sat in silence as it made a slow descent down to the station.

They arrived amid a crush of activity as people were departing the latest arrival. After buying a ticket, Sara was able to board immediately. But before doing so, she turned to give her relatives one final embrace.

"Thank you. Thank you for everything. I had a wonderful time," Sara said earnestly.

"Oh, we're glad you did. Now, don't forget to come for a visit after you're a big-time career girl," Ted said, his eyes crinkled with laughter beneath his furry hat.

Turning, Sara took Mary's hands in hers.

"Mary, you've always been like a mother to me. I can't thank you enough for your advice."

"We've all been where you are, at some time or another. Just hang in there. It will begin to make sense," Mary said, her lips quivering slightly.

After a quick kiss, Sara grabbed her bag, and headed for the train steps. She waved once more before disappearing within the passenger trains interior. It took her a few minutes to find a seat, and the trains whistle sounded off just as she sat down. With a sudden lurch, Sara's journey began.

***

Ed Olson sat hunched over a crackling AM radio.

"This is KRVN with a weather bulletin. The National Weather Service has issued a blizzard advisory for all of Nebraska. A blizzard of dangerous proportions has immobilized much of northern Wyoming and southern South Dakota, causing all major roads to be closed. The storm is expected to continue to track southeasterly at about five miles per hour. This slow-moving storm has dumped more than three feet of blowing snow in parts of Wyoming and South Dakota. All people in the state of Nebraska are advised to take appropriate measures to prepare."

Ed jumped to his feet, donning a heavy coat and pair of knee-high rubber boots. Jumping into his pickup, he quickly drove to a pasture three miles away. There, he found John, who was standing atop a flatbed breaking bales for hungry cattle.

"Looks like we'd better get'em home. Bad blizzard heading for us," Ed said, pulling on a pair of gloves.

"How long have we got?," John said, his forehead burdened with concern.

"It's just reached the panhandle. We should still have several hours. But we've got to get the herd in from the far northwest range. There's no protection, and we've got too many out there," Ed said.

John spotted Zeke on horseback, and motioned for him to come closer. When he was just in hearing range, John began to shout.

"We'll have to move'em out. Storm's com'in. As soon as we get these in, we'll have to bring in the northwest herd."

"Okay, boss. Open the gate, and I'll get 'em," Zeke said, reining his horse sharply.

John knew there was reason to move fast. He'd been through many of these storms in the past. Neighbors had been known to lose whole herds when they became blinded by snow. It was a cows nature to follow the wind, even if it led them to their death. Many times animals would come up a fence, squeezing together until the smaller animals suffocated. The larger animals would continue to battle the snow, sometimes becoming entombed within it's cold, wet fury.

Unhooking the flatbed, John crawled atop the tractor and drove it to the gate. Once opened, he blocked the gravel road going west, forcing the animals to head towards home. As Zeke herded the animals out of the pasture, Ed stayed ahead of the herd, luring them with a few broken hay bales in his open truck box.

Almost all of the cattle knew their way home, having had made the journey several times in the past. On cue, they turned down the long lane leading to the Olson home. With a little coaxing from John, the large beasts turned neatly into the waiting corral.

In unison, the three men turned to head back out the driveway for the more distant and larger pasture. John parked his tractor, and saddled a seasoned chestnut mare. Heading out the driveway, he saw his mother, bundled in a warm, tattered coat and calf-high rubber overshoes, get into the pickup with Joe.

"It's a good idea," John thought to himself, "It's going to take all of us to get them moving."

When they reached the pasture, the cattle were no place in sight. Zeke and John set off on horseback in search of the herd. When they finally found them, the animals were scattered over a 40-acre section in the ranches most distant corner.

The cattle were uncooperative, unwilling to move from their spots. They were considerably more wild than the first bunch. Because of their location, the herd had little contact with humans or confinement. Once John got a few pair moving in the right direction, they suddenly turned, backtracking to their original spots.

Together, Zeke and John were finally able to get the herd rounded up and moving. But progress was slow. John could feel the temperature edging downward. Glancing to the north, he saw ominous black clouds forming along the horizon.

Two hours after they began, the ranchers had almost coaxed the cattle out of the pasture. The gate was in sight. But as the herd got nearer, they saw Joe moving near his pickup. Several of the animals spooked, retracing their steps and setting John and Zeke's efforts back by almost half a mile.

By the time the cattle reached the gate, the dark clouds had risen, forming a seemingly impenetrable wall in the heavens. A sharp wind began beating at John's exposed flesh, battering his cheeks until they turned red.

Once the cattle hit the gravel road, they began running ahead full speed, passing up Ed and Helen in their hay-laden vehicle. Ed's truck belched out a cloud of acidic, black soot as he pushed the accelerator hard to stay ahead. They answered by fleeing in all directions. A few young animals squeezed through neighbors fences and wandered away from the herd. John left Zeke to follow up from the rear as he rounded up the runaways.

Eventually, the animals calmed down as they slowed to munch on a few brittle strands of exposed roadside grass. Ed and Helen crept ahead with the pickup, eventually interesting a few animals in following them. Soon, the other cattle followed and were led to the Olson driveway.

To ensure the animals turned into the driveway, Helen got out of the pickup and guided the cattle into the lane as Ed continued on with his lure. Getting out of his pickup, he opened the corral gate and escorted the animals in.

As the last few cattle rounded the driveway, John brought in the spirited strays. They were lively young steers, occasionally kicking up their hind legs in protest as they headed down the lane.

Finally, the last calf rounded the bend and made his way for the open corral. John was just about to breath a sigh of relief when he stopped dead in his tracks. He watched as Ed rushed forward, grasp the gate in both hands and quickly move to close it. Just as he was about to secure the latch, a young bull decided to make one final protest. In a flash he threw out both hind legs, striking the gate boards squarely. The sound of cracking wood resonated as Ed was thrown back from the impact. In a single motion the senior Olson fell backwards, landing hard on his back.

In a flash Zeke, John and Helen were by Ed's side. He laid there for a moment, stunned and winded from the blow. Zeke grabbed the creaking, now-broken gate and in a quick motion bound it closed with a length of bailing wire.

Helen knelt by Ed's head, using her legs to support her husband's head.

"Dad, can you talk?," John said, frantically searching his father's face.

After a few seconds, Ed brought his hand to his forehead, touching it gingerly. "Yes. Fine. Just caught me off guard," he said.

"Does anything hurt? Do you have pain?," Helen asked, placing her face over Ed's to shield it from the wind.

"No." Ed used his arms to brace himself, lifting his head from Helen's thighs and drawing himself into a seated position. "No. Everything feels okay. I'm just a little shook up."

Ed attempted to stand up, but lost his balance and fell into his son's outstretched arms.

"We'd better have the doctor take a look. You took quite a blow," Helen said, her arm encircling Ed's waist.

John joined her, supporting Ed's other arm. Together, they brought him to the passenger-door of the pickup and helped him in. As John slammed the door shut, he turned to his mother.

"I don't think it's anything serious, but I'd better get moving to beat the storm," he said.

"Yes, you go right away. I'll get dressed and Zeke and I will follow you into town," Helen said, walking for the house.

John immediately got into the drivers seat and maneuvered the pickup down the driveway. As he reached the main road, the first few flakes of snow began drifting down from the murky gray sky.

Five miles into his journey, the wind began to pick up considerably. The innocent white puffs of snow turned into a white froth that slapped against the windshield and clung there selfishly until being swept away by frantic windshield wipers. John strained to see the road before him, and was relieved to make out the North Platte city limit sign.

As he turned the car toward the hospital, John realized he arrived in town just in time. A thin layer of ice was beginning to form on the road, making travel almost impossible.

John helped his father into the emergency room. A nurse immediately took his blood pressure and reported that, at least, was normal. However, an ugly purple welt was forming on Ed's forehead. An on-staff doctor peered into his eyes with a light, and ordered some X-rays be taken.

As Ed was wheeled to a different room, John heard his name being paged on the intercom. Making his way to the nurses station, he was handed the telephone. His mother's frantic voice answered.

"John. How's dad?"

"They just took him down to X-ray. The doctor think's it's a concussion, but they just want to make sure. They'll probably want to keep him overnight."

"I don't think we're going to make it. The car stalled in the driveway. It was snowing so hard we almost couldn't find our way back to the house."

"It may be better for you to sit tight. Dad's in good hands, and the doctor didn't give me the impression he's very concerned. Anyway, the roads into town are getting slick."

"As soon as you know anything, give me a call. I want to know exactly what's going on," Helen said.

As he hung up, John glanced out a large window facing the parking lot. He noticed it was difficult to see the end of the sidewalk, which didn't extend more than fourty feet from the front door. Cars parked outside were already blanketed with about three inches of the heavy white stuff.

John paced the otherwise abandoned waiting room impatiently. After a time he surrendered and sat down, anxiety drumming in his stomach. The wait seemed endless. But eventually, a white-coated doctor entered the room.

"Well, John, looks like your dad's going to be fine—maybe a little sore for awhile though. The X-ray's don't show any serious damage. He'll need to stay a couple of days for observation." The doctor motioned to the window. "And by the looks of it outside, I'd imagine you'll be our guest tonight, as well. Your dad's being moved to a room now, so you'll be able to see him shortly," the doctor said as he made his way out the door.

"Thank God," John muttered under his breath. Walking over to the window, he crossed his arms, and watched the snow pelt down mercilessly.

***

Sara had spotted the angry mass of clouds in the distance, and watched them with interest as her train drew closer. At first, she thought they looked beautiful, like a rich, luxurious lace trimming the horizon. But as she got closer, a sense of fear began forming in her breast. The sky became dark and frightening, as if God's wrath was being played out in the heavens.

As the train crossed into Nebraska, the first flakes began to fly half-hazardly from an eerie green sky. A stern north wind pushed against the train's windows, whistling as it squeaked through loose-fitting panes.

Half an hour later, the train was forced to slow down. The conductor was unable to see more than a few hundred feet in front of the train. Gusts of wind pushed at the heavy iron cars, testing their weight. Slowly, the locomotive pushed on, a burdened caterpillar inching ever closer to its destination.

To Sara, it seemed like hours had passed when a small sign indicated the town of Sutherland was approaching. As the train inched to a stop, she strained to make out the city. Darkness had blanketed the area, leaving only the outline of a few building visible. Cars dotted the main street, their tires almost buried by the swirling snow.

Passengers within the train had been subdued throughout most of the journey from Colorado. But as the train sat a dull murmur began to arise. Sara caught bits and pieces of conversations being batted back and forth anxiously.

"Haven't seen a storm like this since..."

"Expecting to be there, but doesn't look like ..."

"Do you think we'll keep going, or ..."

After several minutes, word circulated the engineer was getting information on storm conditions. Squinting her eyes, she could just barely make out the figures of three men in a depot across the tracks. The manager stood at his post, one arm resting on the counter before him, the other moving back and forth dramatically as he spoke.

Across from him stood a man who appeared to be a train engineer, the collar of his heavy coat gathered around his neck. He shuffled from leg to leg, tugging nervously at his hat, then his ear, while listening to the manager. Another man, this one considerably younger than the others, stood by the conductor with crossed arms. Every so often, he would nod his head in understanding. His attention turned first to one man, then the other, listening intently as each took a turn speaking.

The scene went on for quite some time. Sara saw the trio's serious demeanor dissolve briefly, a shared joke bringing brief laughter. The conductor and his young apprentice made a move for the door. A final brief wave and the duo stepped out the depot door.

The two men braced noticeably as a cold, bitter wind battered their coats. The elder firmly stuck his hands into his pockets and made his way to for the engine. His young helper clutched the brim of his flat derby hat and trotted along side.

A few slow minutes elapsed. Sara felt an icy draft slither between her ankles. Her feet had gradually gotten colder and colder. She tried to wiggle her toes in her shoes to ward off the numbness creeping into her feet. Sara pulled her coat close and rubbed her arms nervously.

With a lurch the train set off again, it's whistle sounding off a nervous shriek. Ever so slowly the towns lights passed into the distance. They were replaced by hollow, unrelenting wind and a vast nothingness that unnerved the young New Yorker. She felt imprisoned within the trains confines. The other passengers offered little comfort. Like her, they felt minuscule, caught up in something much larger and more powerful. The evenings threat loomed heavily, daring each to try their fate in an unwinable battle.

In a scared whisper, word of the evenings fate began circulating among the trains passengers. To be sure it appeared to Sara as if the train was barely moving at times.

Finally, the young man Sara observed talking in the depot appeared at the front of the car.

"Ladies and gentlemen, the engineer has sent me back to tell you we will be stopping in North Platte to wait out the storm. Prepare to get off the train at that time. Facilities are being readied for our stay."

Sara breathed out a sigh of relief. Tired and cold, she had had enough of this journey through Nebraska's darkness. She was ready to return to the comfort of home, and pitied those who chose to make their home in such a desolate, God forsaken land.

***

John sat beside his father until he drifted off to sleep. After a time he became aware of a good deal activity in the hallway. Meandering out to stretch his legs, he caught a nurses attention as she swept by with an armful of neatly folded blankets.

"My, you're busy this evening. Has there been an accident?," John asked.

"No, but we're bracing for a lot of activity," the nurse answered hurriedly. "Several cars have been stranded, and a shelter is being set up in the auditorium down the block. They've sent out a call for volunteers. The hospital was asked to provide any extra pillows or blankets we can spare, so that's what we're doing now."

"How many inches of snow have fallen?"

"Last I heard about a foot, and it's coming down hard with the wind. In fact, it's bad enough to stop train travel. We got word of at least two lines that will be stopping here in town to wait out the storm. It's a real mess."

"Sounds bad all right."

Glancing at her watch, the nurse turned to go. "Just be glad you're here instead of out there," she said over her shoulder.

John walked toward the lobby. "I wonder how things are going at home?," he wondered to himself. Looking outside, he was taken aback. In the past hour, the situation had changed dramatically. Snow had already erased the streets and created flowing bridges between store fronts. No cars were moving, although the faint image of a figure trudging down the street could be made out.

Picking up a pay phone, John dropped in his change and dialed. After a single ring, his mother answered.

"Hello?" her anxious voice chirped.

"Hello. It's me. How are things going?"

"Fine here, how about there?"

"Good. Dad's asleep, I think for the night. The streets are really bad here. It doesn't look like I'll be going anyplace for awhile."

"You don't need to worry about things here. Zeke got the smaller calves put in the barn. The tank heater's started so they've got plenty of water. We've done all we can for now."

"Okay, I guess I'll let you go, then. Just don't try doing anything outside on your own. If there's a problem just let Zeke know."

"Yes. And you take good care of you're father."

John hung up the phone, relieved to have heard his mother's voice. Just then, a blast of cold air entered the room as the hospital's door flew open. A group of about 40 people began crowding into the previously abandoned hospital lobby. A man who appeared to be leading them made his way to the nurses station.

Coming near, John heard the man explain the situation in muffled tones. The school auditorium was filled, and organizers had instructed the group to wait at the hospital. Requests for people to open their homes to the stranded travelers had been sent out. But until something was heard, the hungry and exhausted travelers from Colorado would have to stay put.

Immediately, the nurses snapped into action. Going from room to room, unused chairs were brought into the lobby, as were the few spare blankets and pillows still available. The hospital had no cafeteria, so a nurse slipped into a small break room staff used for lunch. A short time later, she came out with trays of hot chocolate and coffee the weary travelers graciously accepted.

John pitched in where he could, helping the group settle in and be as comfortable as possible. Requests by the nurses kept him on his toes. After about an hour, a group of five men swept into the lobby carrying containers of delicious-spelling food and a large kettle of warm soup.

A large, robust man leading the men got the attention of the stranded travelers by raising his hands.

"Ladies and gentlemen, we are members of the local fire department. Some of the good ladies in the community heard about your dilemma and whipped up a few goodies in their kitchens for you to enjoy. We've got soup, sandwiches and a couple casseroles for you to chow down on. If we could get a few volunteers to help serve this up, the rest of you can start forming a line and we'll get this show on the road."

Chairs began to shuffle as the hungry and relieved group began gathering. Among them was Sara, who could sense the groups fatigue and anxiety. Stepping up to the nurses station, which had become a half-hazard cafeteria line, she offered her services. A harried nurse gratefully accepted her help and directed her towards several large sandwich containers.

"Just keep those trays full, honey," the nurse directed as she sped down the hall to care for a patient.

Another nurse tapped John, who was leaning up against a wall, on the shoulder.

"If you don't mind, I was wondering if you'd help dish out the soup," she said apologetically.

John nodded, and took his place in the serving line.

One by one, plates were filled and distributed. John couldn't help but notice the pretty young traveler cheerfully helping by his side. Despite her trying experience, she had a smile and pleasant word for almost all of her fellow passengers. Like the others, she must have been tired and hungry, yet she seemed amazingly oblivious to her own discomfort.

As the line began to wane, John spoke gingerly.

"The line is almost done. Would you like to get a plate for yourself and sit down? I'm sure somebody else could take your place if you're getting tired."

"Oh, no. But thanks. I actually think I'm too nervous to eat, anyway. It was kind of a stressful journey."

"Are you from Colorado?," John asked, her choppy northeastern accent throwing him off.

Tucking a curly brown strand of hair behind her ear, Sara laughed. With an amused, sideways glance, she pursed her lips.

"Why no, as a matter of fact, I'm not."

Sara went on to tell John about her Colorado visit. She talked at length about her aunt and uncle's mountainside home. As she went on, Sara was surprised at how easy it was to talk to John. He appeared to be reserved, yet expressed an interest in what she said. Aware of the attention John offered, Sara went on to relay the story of her trying train journey which brought her to North Platte.

"Really, I've just never seen anything like this before. Do you get storms like this often?," Sara asked.

By now, the duo was done serving food. Filling their own plates, they made their way to a single vacant chair in the crowded waiting room.

"Well, they aren't usually this bad," John said, "but we do get our share of snow every now and then."

"And so, how is it that you got stuck in a hospital, of all places?," Sara said.

"My dad, actually. He's a patient here. Had a run in with an ornery calf just as the snow began to fly."

"Oh my God!," Sara's eyes opened wide in surprise. "Your dad's ill in this hospital, and you've been out here fretting over some wayward travelers?"

"Turns out he was lucky. Just got a bump on the head. He's resting, now, and I'm sure he'll be fine. I'm just worried about how things are going at home. We are in the cattle business, and a storm like this could seriously jeopardize our herd."

"A cattle man. Hummm," Sara said, rubbing her chin curiously. "You mean, a rancher. How interesting. I don't believe I've ever had the pleasure of meeting a rancher before—much less seeing an actual ranch. That must be an interesting life."

"Well, I don't know if interesting is the word, exactly." John smiled widely at Sara. "But it does keep me out of trouble."

"So, what, exactly, draws a person to be a rancher and live out here in the middle of nowhere? How did you decide on such an occupation?," Sara asked.

Initially, John was stunned by the directness of her question. Not even he fully understood what drew him back to his childhood home. But, haltingly, John began to explain how his decision had come to pass after returning from the service.

He talked of spending endless hours at sea where he never felt completely at home. As John considered his life, he described his appreciation for the land and the many wonders it held. The simple things, like a beautiful sunrise or the joy in seeing a newborn calf struggle to its feet came to mind. Some of God's most significant wonders that could easily be missed or taken for granted. ·

John realized that he had never put his feelings into words, or, for that matter, fully realized the origin of his feelings. His thoughts had come flooding out. When he finished, John was taken aback by all that he'd revealed. After all, this girl was a complete stranger who he knew nothing about. But perhaps, John thought, she was just the catalyst he needed. She appeared interested, yet was someone he may never see again. John pulled himself to his feet.

"Well, I'm sure that's more of an answer than you expected to get. Now I think I'd better go look in on my father."

Sara studied John's as he disappeared down the hall. "What an odd man," she thought. "He's given such a good deal of thought to things most people don't even consider. Odd, that such insights would come from someone living in such a God-forsaken place.

Sara sat there for a few moments, contemplating the man she'd met. A most interesting person, to be sure, she thought. As she glanced out of the night-darkened sky, flakes of heavy snow continued to patter insistently at the window pane.

After checking on his father, who was sound asleep, John peered out of his hospital window at the same snow. He watched as it sifted down from the sky, only to be swept up by a persistent north wind.

John's thoughts shifted to his mother and the ranch. Striding the the hall, John once again picked up the phone, only to be greeted with a hollow, empty silence. He realized the telephone lines must have come down, and any chance for communication was lost. All he could do was hope Zeke and his mother could handle what lay ahead.

Chapter 5

"Time to get up, sleepy head."

John awoke with a start. He had drifted off to sleep in a chair beside his father's bed. Immediately, a stabbing pain shot through his neck, evidence of a hard nights sleep.

"Rise and shine, John Olson."

John looked up to see Sara standing in the doorway. His father stirred slightly in his bed.

The room appeared dark, with snow firmly packed into the window screen.

"What time is it," John answered wearily.

"It's 7:30 in the morning. And we are on breakfast detail," Sara answered cheerily.

On their way down to the nurses station, Sara quickly filled John in. Electricity was out in most of the area, as was telephone service. Electricity in the hospital, high school gymnasium, and other buildings in town was being supplied by generators. Red Cross volunteers who had brought in food informed the stranded travelers that most of the state was also affected, with more than three feet of snow on the ground.

And weather reports indicated the worst was still to come. Two more days of snow were expected by the National Weather Service. As winds continued to howl across the prairie, drifts were swept up on roads, preventing travel and threatening to smother unprotected animals.

After the meals were dished out, Sara handed John a plate. "Why don't we have breakfast with your dad?," she suggested.

As John peered into the room, he was relieved to see his father sitting up. One of the nurses had delivered a tray of food and he appeared to be looking it over as John and Sara entered.

"It's nice to see you're finally awake. You had a nice long nap," John said as he moved to sit on the edge of the bed.

"Yes, I hear I missed quite a bit of commotion. Have you checked with mom to see how things are going?"

"Not since late last night," John said. "And the lines are down now, so I guess we'll just have to have faith everything is working out."

"And who is this pretty young guest you've brought?," Ed said, nodding politely to Sara.

Extending her hand, Sara walked towards Ed. "Hello. My name is Sara Morris. My train got stranded, and the local people were kind enough to make some room available for us here. Your son has been helping out and showing us all a good deal of your local hospitality," she said.

Ed reached out to accept Sara's hand, while smiling broadly. "I'm very pleased that you've come to pay me a visit. Go ahead and have a seat," he said, motioning to the vacant chair John had slept in during the night.

"So when is the storm supposed to let up," Ed asked.

John shrugged as he popped a forkful of eggs into his mouth. "Sounds like the snow could last two more days. But we might be in for quite a wait before getting home. Sounds like the wind keeps blowing the roads closed. Everything is shut down."

Ed pushed his plate aside and twined his fingers together thoughtfully.

"I'm sure Zeke and your mother have their hands full. We had some hay put up in the barn, but I doubt that will be enough to last more than about four days. Hopefully by then they'll be able to get to the hay stack we made on the northwest 40. That one would last several weeks."

"It might be completely buried by the snow," John said.

Sara listened to their conversation with interest. She had never been in a battle with nature before. She shuddered to think of the influence the weather had on the lives of these people, not to mention it's affect on their financial well-being.

The trio sat together well after their meals were finished. Ed asked Sara about her life in far away New York. She obliged by talking about her parents and some of the activities they engaged in for fun and entertainment. When Sara said that her father was an avid golfer, Ed shook his head.

"I just really don't understand the game. It seems like a lot of time devoted to something with little reward."

"He likes the challenge, I think. And it's his time to make business connections while having a little fun," Sara said.

John considered the idea of ones financial success being dependent on their ability to socialize successfully. It seemed like a tiring project, so unlike the solitary way of life he found comfort in.

Eventually, Sara and John gathered up their dishes and set off down the hall. The Red Cross volunteers had brought games, decks of cards and magazines to help the stranded travelers pass time. Sara snatched up a deck at waved them at John.

"So, are you up for a game of Old Maid?," she said, laughing.

The two spent most of the next two days together, unlikely companions thrown together by factors beyond their control. They drifted between Ed's room and that of the weary travelers. Sometimes, the two opted to go their separate ways and visit with some of the other travelers. But inevitably, the two would meet up again, anxious to repeat the latest bit of news they had heard about the storm that held so many in its icy grip.

Beyond the hospitals walls, wind continued to push snow into rock-hard mountains. Residents within the small Nebraska panhandle town bonded together to serve the needs of stranded travelers. In addition to the hospital, schools, churches and private homes were made available during the storm.

Outside the city, all life drew to a halt. Snow drifts up to 40 inches high and half a mile long snaked their way across the open land. Strong winds blew roads shut behind road crews valiantly attempting to make them passable. Both man and beast were threatened by the sub-zero temperatures. Cattle with no shelter became entrapped by the snow, suffocating in it's swirling rage. And so it went, for three long days.

On the fourth day , John awoke with a start in his usual position along side his father's hospital bed. Maneuvering to work the now-familiar knot from his back, his eyes fell upon an empty bed. His father was standing beside the window. He was dressed in a striped hospital robe which was wound around him tightly.

John blinked, shielding his eyes from an unfamiliar sight. The sun was out in full glory, basking in winter's white blanket flowing over the earth. John leapt to his feet and joined his father to survey what nature had left in its wake.

Cars parked along the street were buried. Wind had whipped the snow into grills and between loose-fitting doors. A few large, strong men were in front of their stores, surveying the scene. One buried a shovel in the mound, and with obvious effort lifted it slightly, tossing in a few inches away. Again he tried, this time with more force. Again, the heavy stuff resisted, clinging to his shovel as he tried to propel it into the air.

"This sure is going to set us back," Ed said, shaking his head. "I'll bet we won't have a head standing."

"Don't be so sure. Zeke's a good man. And we did get the herds home. That will make a big difference," John said, reassuringly.

"One things for sure—I can't take any more of this laying around. It's time to start moving." Looking from side to side, Ed appeared momentarily flustered. "Where in the world are my clothes?"

As John made his way into the hospital's waiting room, it appeared the same restlessness was gripping all those held captive during the storm. On one side of the room, the men paced anxiously, alternately glancing at watches and discussing the days turn of events. On the other side of the room, women straightened their clothes and combed hair, as if awakening from a long slumber.

A nurse sat at the station absentmindedly tapping a pencil on the desk. John caught her attention as he neared.

"It looks as if you'll be losing your guests soon," he said.

"Not quite yet, I'm afraid," she answered wryly. "Most of these people think just because the sun is out their train will be pulling up any second to whisk them away. Well, I'm here to tell you it's not going to happen. The snow's four feet high where it isn't drifted, and a lot worse where it has. Snows everywhere. No, that train's not pull'in out for awhile," she said.

As usual, the Red Cross delivered food right on time. Everybody looked forward to these visits, and greeted those who brought the warm food as old friends. On their way out, men gave them hearty hand shakes and encouraging pats on the back. Women listened in attentively for any news these messengers from the outside world could provide.

At breakfast, John was joined by his father, dressed in clean clothes someone had been kind enough to wash and press in the midst of the snowy drama. Sara briefly joined them. But after a short time she drifted away to visit with some fellow travelers.

While the storm had raged outside, the hospital had become like a world of its own for the New York woman. It offered refuge from the fear and uncertainty of what was taking place outside. She had shared something with those in the building—a sense of surviving something awesome—a power released from God's regal hand.

And John had been a part of that world. His life and perspectives were foreign to Sara. Like the storm bluntness, his viewpoints offered a sense of purity and realism she was oblivious to before. His simple life, and the pleasure he derived from that simplicity was fresh and alluring to the girl searching for answers.

But as the sun shone, the subtle intimacy the storm created fluttered away like a wounded sparrow searching for cover. The common thread uniting the group began to unravel, and John's life was a world away from her day to day concerns. The days brightness seemed to shine a harsh spotlight on their different lifestyles. While she found John interesting, the sun's piercing light seemed to point out the need for her to resume her own life, and grapple with the problems she had abandoned with ease just days ago.

It seemed imperative to once again connect with the world she knew. And Sara realized that cohesion did not rest with John, but her fellow passengers. Like her, they were simply visitors in this place. Their lives extended far beyond this small Nebraska town to a place in the distance where the railroad tracks disappear on the horizon.

John's interest has also changed. His concerns laid just down the road, where family and a demanding occupation were bidding him to come home. After he finished eating breakfast, he donned a winter coat and headed for the hospital's door.

Despite the bitterly-cold temperatures, John breathed in the fresh, clean air. It was a welcome change from the hospital's stagnant odor. Snow crunched beneath his boots and swallowed his legs as he made his way down the street. After trudging six blocks, he turned toward a familiar house. Knocking on the door briskly, the door flew open and his old friend Fred appeared.

"John? How in the devil did you get here?," Fred said in amazement.

"It's a long story, but I got snowed in. I've been riding the storm out at the hospital."

Just then, Fred's mother poked her head out of the kitchen.

"Don't just stand there letting out the warm air, let John in and shut the door. John, how are you doing? Why didn't you come here during the storm?," she asked

"Well, my dad got worked over pretty good by a calf and had to be admitted. He's fine now, but I figured I'd stay with him," John said.

"I'm glad you stopped by. Are you hungry? Lucky for me, we kept our old wood cook stove from my mother. The old things been keeping us warm and it's the only way to cook anything since the electricity is out."

"Thanks, I'm fine. But I did want to put your son to work. I was wondering if you still had your old HAM radio going?"

"Oh. Sure, it's still set up. I guess I kind of forgot about it."

"Well, with any luck I might be able to get a hold of mom. She's been out at the farm alone all this time. Except for Zeke of course. I hope he didn't drive her crazy," John said.

John followed Fred to a back room, where the radio was slid into a bookshelf. After tinkering with some wires, he handed John the receiver.

"Good luck," he said.

John brought the mouthpiece to his face.

"John Olson to Helen Olson. Helen Olson, are you there?"

Immediately, there was a crackle and then the voice of his mother came through the machine in muffled tones.

"John, I'd hoped you'd make your way to a radio. I dug ours out two days ago hoping you'd remember we had it and try to call. How's your father?"

"Fine, he's doing good and ready to go home. How are things there?"

"Well, I've seen better. We lost quite a few calves. Zeke had his hands full trying to get them fed. Now that the storm's died down, he's hoping to take the tractor out to the haystack and bring some feed back. It's going to be a mess for awhile."

The radio crackled, then wined loudly.

"We'll do our best to get home as soon as possible. But it may take some time," John said.

Standing up, John made his way to the front door.

"Thanks a lot, Fred. I'm going to try and find the road crew. Maybe they could use a little extra help."

After trudging through the snow for another eight blocks, John spotted the large county maintenance shed. Two of the maintainers were gone, and one sat idling in the shed.

"Hello!" John shouted over the engines rumble. "Having any luck?"

An older man who had been adjusting the snowplows blade turned toward John and leaned on one of the machines large rubber wheels.

"Oh, we're moving right along. But it's slow going. The snows drifted pretty bad in some spots," he said.

"Could you use some help?," John offered

"Sure. You can help me finish getting this put on. You could even ride along if you want. Seems like I always need help dragging fallen trees off the road," the man said.

55

So it came to pass that for the next three days, John helped the road crew. But progress was slow and conditions on the open prairie were brutal. Strong north winds continued to blow snow across roads. Sub-zero temperatures numbed Johns fingers and toes as he helped to remove fallen trees and stalled vehicles from main roadways.

John had seen significant snow storms before. But in all his years, he had never witnessed one of such severity. In all directions, at least 30 inches of snow blanketed the ground. Huge drifts extended as far as the eye could see. Snow plows proved to be no match for nature's fury. Rock hard and unforgiving, they resisted the efforts of lumbering snow plows.

Time after time, the huge mechanical beasts backed up, then charged forward in an attempt to claim victory. But each time, progress of only a foot or two was made. Crews would persist, continuing again and again.

Like a rodent tunneling through the ground, walls of snow extending several feet high would form as the snow grudgingly gave way. With a final burst of exuberance the maintainer would make one final run. At last, snow would explode into the air as a sign of submission. So it would go, again and again.

The situations severity was recognized statewide. Road crews received word the governor had activated the National Guard. Army personnel were also dispatched to the area in a massive effort that would soon be known as Operation Snowbound.

Completely cut off from civilization, medical supples were flown out to ranchers in need. Feed for cattle was completely buried, and animals began to die of starvation. In a desperate effort to save them, pilots would fly overhead, dropping hay where needed.

After four days, damage estimates began trickling in. It was believed the storm had stranded 85,000 people and taken the lives of more than 100. Livestock fared poorly, with about 65 thousand cattle and 45 thousand sheep reported lost.

Each night, John would return to town and the sanctuary of the hospital. By that time, his muscles ached and the buildings soothing warmth was a welcome relief. He would talk to his father and Sara briefly. But exhaustion would soon overtake him and he would drift into a deep, sound slumber until morning would come.

Nervousness had driven John's father outdoors during the day as well. He did his part to help with snow efforts around town. Ed had recuperated to the point where he could shovel small amounts of snow, but the cold weather kept him at bay. Instead, his efforts were focused on helping to keep the stranded travelers comfortable. So he waited, ever so impatiently.

But even many of the travelers were getting involved in cleanup efforts. Bitten by cabin fever and the desire to be on their way, many of Sara's fellow train travelers were focusing on helping the railroad resume operations. Several crews were formed to help clear the line. But like the road workers, progress was frustratingly slow.

Finally, ten days after the storm ended, the first signs of progress were realized. John awoke with a start when a sound he hadn't heard in days faintly made its way through the chilled Nebraska air. Moments later, he heard it again—the proud, strong call of a train whistle.

Immediately, John found his feet and made his way to the hospital lobby. The passengers were milling about anxiously, gathering their belongings and tugging on gloves. Searching the crowd, he caught sight of Sara and quickly made his way in her direction.

"What's all the action about?," John asked somberly, still groggy from sleep.

"Haven't you heard?," Sara said as she buttoned her coat. "The train engineer is going to give it a try. He got word that most of the track to the east had been cleared."

"Why, that's good news. Maybe you'll beat me home," John said as he glanced out a window to the snowy terrain.

Sara extended her hand. "John, it's been a pleasure getting to know you. Perhaps we'll come across each other again some time."

John smiled, knowing the possibility was unlikely. Still, he nodded in agreement. Suddenly, he was struck by an idea.

"You know, we could stay in touch. Drop me a line by mail when you get a chance. I'd like to hear how you're doing," John said.

Sara's eyes lit up. "John, maybe you could come out to New York for a visit some time. After all, I've spent all this time in Nebraska. You could surely give New York a look." Sara saw doubt cloud Johns face, as he recalled his war-time experiences on the coast. As if reading his mind, she countered quickly. "Oh, come on! I could be your tour guide. It would be fun."

For a second, John could see himself in New York, with Sara by his side. His previous experience in the big city had left a negative impression. But he was alone, then, in a town where he didn't fit in. Perhaps with someone he knew, things would be different.

With a sheepish grin, John cast his eyes to the ceiling. "Well, that could be interesting. But if I do that, you'll have to return to Nebraska and see what a rancher's life is really like—when we aren't buried under a ton of snow."

"Sounds like a deal, then," Sara said, extending her hand again. "Goodbye, John Olson. I'll be seeing you again."

With that, she swept out the hospital door, turning to wave briefly before disappearing into the frozen world outside. Several minutes later, the train's whistle sounded again. Dunning his boots and warm woolen jacket, John plodded toward the train just as it started to move away from the station. As he got closer, he caught sight of Sara's image in a snow-framed window. Squinting as the sun's rays bounced from the white snow, he waved heartily as Sara nodded. Like a serpent the train rumbled away and slipped from sight as it disappeared over the horizon.

Walking back to his father, John passed through the now-vacant hospital lobby. It seemed odd, and a little sad after being crowded with people for so long. John thought about the pledge that he and Sara had just made.

"Probably just idle words," he muttered to himself. "It will soon be forgotten when she gets back to her own world."

With the train's departure, it seemed as though things began moving quickly in the city of North Platte. After Sara's train pulled away from the station, three more passed though, each taking with them several carloads of passengers. Soon, only those who were traveling by car and locals like John and his father were left.

Even that changed. One day later, crews made progress in bulldozing through to the Olson ranch. Upon hearing the news, John and Ed immediately got in their pickup and headed in the direction of home.

Ed became increasingly agitated as he saw the condition of the countryside. While John had been out working with road crews, Ed had stayed within the confines of the city and could only guess at conditions beyond the city limits. John maneuvered the truck over snow-packed roads and between narrow pathways drilled by weary maintainers.

Ed repeatedly shook his head in disgust.

"We'll be lucky if anything was saved. It just doesn't look good at all," he said.

It took almost an hour before John and Ed traveled the ten mile route home. When they finally reached their driveway, they saw that Zeke had cleared the way with a tractor and loader.

As John killed the pickup motor, Helen appeared in the doorway of the house. Sticking her head out, she shouted loudly.

"Just look at what happens when I let you two go into town! Get in here before supper gets cold!"

John couldn't have felt more relieved as he entered the familiar old kitchen. The wood-burning stove was fully stoked and provided welcomed warmth in an otherwise cold house. It would no doubt be some time before electricity and telephone service was returned.

Helen quickly brought the men up to speed on the events of the past two weeks. Rather than try moving the cattle through drifts, Zeke attempted to bring hay in from a stack located about two miles away. Although it took him two days to do it, he was eventually able to move just enough to keep the animals from starving. Even as they spoke, he was attempting to retrieve more bales.

Still, some animals were lost. Although they had worked throughout the blizzard, Zeke and Helen could not prevent the animals on the yard from packing together. Helen estimated that about 10 percent of the herd was lost.

After finishing a cup of coffee, John rose to his feet and headed out the door to do what he could to help Zeke. As he looked out at the barren countryside, thoughts of Sara came back to him. She was a unique person caught in an unbelievable situation. Yes, their lifestyles were starkly different, and the pact they made could well turn into nothing more than idle words. Yet, it would take time to get her out of his mind.

He was jolted from his thoughts by his mother's questioning voice.

"So what did you two do in town these last few weeks?," she said.

"Just played some cards," John shot across his shoulder before disappearing out the front door.

At the same time, hundreds of miles away, Sara's train was inching across the Ohio's eastern border. She was surprised at the number of miles the snow storm had encompassed. Not until reaching Iowa's midsection did the drifts lessen.

It had been a long, hard journey, to be sure. Resting her head upon the train's window, exhaustion seemed to encompass her entire being. "How wonderful it would be to stretch out on a soft, clean bed and sleep for days," she thought to herself.

Still, she couldn't help but contemplate the many contributions others had made during the trying ordeal. It was amazing how total strangers had banded together when needed. The volunteers who had provided the large group of travelers with so many meals during her North Platte stay left Sara with a warm feeling. Young and old, wealthy and poor were equally affected by the natural disaster. Yet, they all managed to pull together when needed.

This was something new for Sara. Many of those she grew up with would have bristled at the notion of working with those of lesser means to get a job done. Sara recognized that many of those offering help and support in North Platte were undergoing extreme pressure themselves. Yet in the storms stressful wake, many discounted the financial and emotional stress they were feeling to focus on others.

Sara's thoughts drifted to John Olson, whose very livelihood hung in the balance throughout the storm. Yet, he was content to stay by his father's side, where his heart rested. Financial concerns paled when compared to the value of human life.

Sara reflected on the time they shared together, telling each other about their lives, playing cards, and making fun to pass the time. "Yes, he's a person I would like to keep in contact with," she thought to herself. "Yet, we have only this storm in common."

Still, she could not forget her promise to meet again. "At the very least, I'll write him. He is a person I would like to remember," she thought.

***

As time passed, the experience of those two weeks got lost in the stuff of everyday life. For both Sara and John, the whole thing seemed to be more like a dream. Classes had already resumed at Sara's college when she returned and she was forced to hit the ground running with her studies.

John, on the other hand, was overwhelmed by the job that lay before him. It would take weeks for the cold, wet snow to disappear. Until that time, feeding and caring for the cattle would prove to be an exhausting full-time job.

When the spring-time sun finally did garner enough strength to reclaim the soil, the storm's full devastation became fully evident. Miles and miles of barbed-wire fence lay down like so much limp, tangled spaghetti. Almost every one of the sturdy wooden posts surrounding the Olson ranch lay flat or broken. Even outbuildings suffered from the storms affects. Strong winds had pulled off shingles and damaged doors, causing John to devote hours to repairs.

Just as John began making headway, calving season hit full force. By then, a hint of green could be seen across the gently-rolling sandhills landscape. Tender blades of grass began emerging from the rich, fertile soil. A sweet, dank odor wafted through the air as a new season breathed life into the barren land.

Throughout his long work days, John often found his mind drifting back into the past, and the incredible two weeks he spent stranded. Sara's smiling face would appear in his mind's eye often as he reflected on those days. She, with her East coast accent and big-city ways. Yet, she had a certain spark — always so full of ideas and the energy to carry them out.

John thought about Sara almost daily. But he realized it was rather unlikely he would ever meet up with the New York girl again.

***

Graduation was less than a month away, and Sara firmly believed it was a month too long.

Her college instructors were busy piling on end-of-year term papers and presenting information for final exams. It seemed to Sara that she spent every free moment in the library with her nose stuck in a book.

It was true, the final weeks of school were burning Sara out. She knew her enthusiasm for college was dismally low. But the truth was, she was ready to get on with her life. While she knew the college experience was of value and one she would reflect on warmly later in life, for now it was more than she could take. The responsibilities and constant deadlines seemed to smother her.

Stressed and bored, she would often catch herself daydreaming about other matters. Time after time, her thoughts would slip back to North Platte. Now, it seemed so long ago. But if she closed her eyes and tried, the feeling of calm she felt there would return. And in the hurricane of her life, the sure and steady eye had a name. It was John Olson.

His calm, quiet manner came back to her, steadying her even when so many miles away. Curling a stray hair around a finger, Sara recalled the hours she spent in North Platte. "Perhaps it wasn't John, as much as it was the circumstances surrounding her stay," she thought. All of the local people seemed to have a calm air of competence around them. They, like the smooth, steady land surrounding them, held no false pretenses about life.

John Olson seemed to personify the areas soft-spoken goodwill. But it was a manner tempered by a solid ruggedness. Yes, it was obvious he was a caring person. But Sara had gotten the impression there was much more below the surface of the North Platte man's nonchalant behavior. His personality was one of many layers that would take time to understand and appreciate.

He was so different from other acquaintances. His home-spun common sense and honest way of looking at things was so different from the other people she knew. Like Mary and Ted, John seemed to have an understanding of life's basics that others lacked, or simply failed to recognize.

Sara thought it would be nice to maintain contact with her new friend, if for no other reason than to better understand his unique perspective. But what would be the best way to do so? Should she initiate a letter? Telephone him? Sara lightly tapped a pencil on her book as she contemplated the matter. Lost in thought, her eyes fell to the book she was reading.

"That's it!," she thought to herself excitedly. "Graduation. I'll just send him an invitation. After, all, he did agree to come for a visit sometime. It would be a great time!"

Sara slammed her book closed and hurriedly gathered her things. Breezing across campus, she headed straight for her room. After throwing her books down on the bed, she made her way to her desk and snatched an invitation from a box. For a moment, she couldn't remember where she had stashed John's address. With a sense of urgency, she began searching under piles of papers strewn about.

Unable to locate it, Sara plopped herself down in the desk's chair and began drumming her fingers, deep in thought. With a start she sat up and headed for her closet. Shoes and boxes began flying as Sara frantically tossed them out. At last, she found it—the satchel she had taken on her trip to Colorado. She thrust her hand inside, flailing about quickly until her hand brushed a lone piece of paper. Walking back to the desk, she unfolded the small scrap on which John had scrawled his mailing address and home phone number.

Seconds later, the envelope was addressed. Before inserting the graduation announcement, Sara grabbed a pen from her desk drawer and scrawled a quick note along the bottom.

"Do you remember our promise?," she wrote in a thin, arching script. Licking the envelope, Sara smiled broadly as she leaned back in her chair. "This will be perfect," she said to herself. "What an excellent idea."

***

"Hold him steady!," Zeke shouted as he brandished a branding iron.

Seconds later, steam and the smell of burned flesh spiced the air. Like a carefully choreographed dance, John let up on the struggling young calf just as the iron was lifted. With a single pull, the rope was released and the animal sprang to its feet and ran to join the rest of the herd.

"How are we doin'?," John asked, breathing heavy from the struggle.

"Good. Only about 30 more," Zeke answered.

Brandishing the rope, John headed back to a holding pen where the calves wined mournfully for their mothers.

After they got their vaccinations and brands, the calves would have received their first rite of passage. With luck, they would grow quickly, flourishing beneath the suns warm summer glow.

By fall, the calves would be separated from their mothers for good. Encouraged by the desire to suck, their cries would continue for days, until their voices were reduced to thin wails, and finally, fell into a fitful silence. As they became more accepting of the grain and crisp hay offered to them, they would lose interest in the nourishment their mothers provided. And quite suddenly, they would cross the threshold into adulthood, oblivious to their former consuming desires.

John had always been fond of the spring. It was a time of rebirth for the countryside and it's inhabitants. For weeks, everything had ground to a halt, imprisoned by winter's oppressive bonds. But the snows that once dominated were no match for life's intense persistency. It burst out from everywhere, consuming winter's fury and softening it into fitful submission.

Zeke and John continued to work the calves for most of the day. As the sun ebbed into the west, it began to cool off quickly. John was grateful to be embraced by the homes warmth.With muscles aching, he dropped himself into a dining room chair beside his father.

Helen walked into the room, carrying a large pot of mashed potatoes. She eyed John's weary shoulders.

"How did you do today?," she asked.

"Good. Got the calves done," John said, fatigue reducing his answer to brief syllables.

"Well, you'd better take it easy. You know, tomorrow is another day," she answered.

"Yes," Ed agreed, "There's nothing wrong with putting in a full day's work. But when you get tired—that's when mistakes are made," he cautioned.

John knew his parents words of caution were well-meant. But the fact was that since his father's accident, Ed's participation on the ranch had dropped dramatically. The experience seemed to make him fragile. His interest in the ranch seemed to drop off as well. Even the heart attack he sustained while John was in the service had not had such a marked effect. But now, John was painfully aware his father was passing the full burden of work upon his shoulders. And whether his parents realized it or not, this would mean many long, hard days ahead.

"You've been so busy, you haven't even had time to look at your mail," Helen said, motioning to a pile on the kitchen counter.

Wearily, John got up. He flipped through several envelopes, most of them bills. At the bottom of the pile was a beige envelope with a rich linen texture. The flourishing, hand-written address was unfamiliar to John. But a quick glance at the return address quickly answered his question. There was only one person he knew in New York.

John grabbed a knife from the silverware drawer and neatly slipped it beneath the envelope flap. His eyes flew over the enclosed announcement. At the bottom, he studied Sara's reminder of their mutual agreement. Walking back to the dining room table, he scanned the invitation for a date.

"May 25. Just what I needed during the busiest time of the year. And it doesn't look like things will improve by then, either," John said to himself.

He ate his meal in silence. The young lady from New York had been in his thoughts since they parted. But as much as he would enjoy seeing her again, the timing seemed off. But how would she take a refusal to such an important event? John knew how hard she had worked at earning a college degree.

Could he somehow make it work? John considered the question at length. Although it was hard for John, he had to admit it was unlikely his father would ever assume his previous interest in the ranch. And Zeke couldn't handle the work load on his own during this busy season.

"John. John, are you with us?," Helen's voice broke through John's thoughts. "John, what in the world has you so distracted? You haven't heard a word I've said.

"Oh. Well, it's nothing. I just got a graduation invitation."

"Do you know someone in this year's high school class?," Helen asked.

"No. Not exactly. The invitation is from a friend. She lives in New York."

"Oh!," Ed said, his face erupting into a huge grin. "I know of a young lady from that area myself. Nice girl. Wouldn't happen to be the same one now, would it?"

"Yep. That would be the one. But I just can't see a way though this. There's just too much going on around here."

Helen studied her son closely. He was still so young in her eyes. Yet his jet-black hair and smooth, unlined face were deceiving. With understanding a mother possesses, she saw before her a young man with a wisdom beyond his years. His strong, muscular arms were evidence of a man with a good work ethic and the determination needed for success.

But as the years had taught her, it would take more than hard work to be successful. While she tried to ignore it, it was becoming obvious she and her husband were growing old. It had been a gradual transition. But now the wheels of time seemed to be hurrying along, sweeping them ever so quickly into the winter of their lives. The pattern's completion would be inevitable. Their days of providing John with some semblance of a family life were quickly running out.

Finding the love of a woman who would stick with John throughout his life, in good times and bad, would be one way of softening the blow. And as a mother hopes for her son, it would also be a way for him to enjoy life's happiness well into the future. Helen wanted John to enjoy life's fruit to the fullest. Only in doing that would he truly know life's full promise of success.

But the path leading John to that goal was up to him. Although tempted to coerce him, Helen held her tongue firmly. She had a smart son. He would do what he felt right.

Having already met Sara, however, Ed was more open to the idea of John traveling to New York.

"Yes, it's a busy time and you have to do what you think. But you might want to consider it. It's not every day you get an invitation from such a nice young lady," he said.

John chuckled at this. He knew Sara was from a family of means. But somehow that got swept away with the snowstorm's bitter winds.

He had honestly never considered Sara's life beyond his experience with her. He could only imagine the culture of those who surrounded her. Surely, they could not be much different. At least her parents must have instilled Sara's acceptance and consideration of others.

But there was really no way he could be sure. And just how important was it for him to learn the answer? Yes, he liked and even admired the bubbly and personable young woman from New York. But was he willing to take it to the next level? Making the trip would make it appear so. John knew he was not normally an outgoing person. He found himself ill-at-ease with unfamiliar people and in new situations.

What would he be saying to Sara if he made the trip? For that matter, what would he be admitting to himself? Would it just be a friendly visit shared between friends? Or would he be opening a new door in their relationship? And if he did make that move, would he be prepared to take the next step in their relationship — whatever that may be?

Later that night, after the dinner dishes were put away and Helen and Ed settled in beside the radio for the evening, John sat beside the table. For a time, he stared at the envelope bearing Sara's graceful script. Absentmindedly, he tapped a pen against the table.

His thoughts and emotions were a jumble, he knew. But of one thing he was certain: the work would not get done without him. And it was the ranch that would have to come first. Yet, he was not prepared to put an end to an ongoing relationship with Sara.

With a steady, even hand, John began his letter to Sara. First, he expressed his regrets, explaining graduation would arrive during ranching's busiest season. He concluded by writing, "however, my invitation to your visiting the ranch still stands." After pausing for just a moment, he added, almost as an afterthought, "Love, John Olson."

"Well, that will probably be the end of that," John said, depositing his letter in the mailbox the next day.

He lifted the red-painted flag on the mailbox, a sign for the mail carrier to stop. Tapping it lightly before he turned to walk down his lane, John silently bid his letter and friendship with Sara farewell.

Chapter 6

Sara awoke the morning of her graduation filled with new promise. It had taken time. Sometimes more that she was willing to give. But in the end, she had succeeded in her goal. And as she stretched out in her bed, the sun falling over her brightly flowered bedspread, a sense of satisfaction tingled throughout her body.

Leaping up, she examined the gown hanging from her closet door and the dress she had carefully chosen for this long-awaited day. "Finally," she thought, "It's over. And time to move on."

Her mother had been busy for weeks, harassing caterers to get just the right menu, pouring over florists catalogs to get the best arrangements. The guest list was something Sara shuddered to even consider. Everyone Sara and her parents knew were invited. Agnes had missed no one. Everyone from old grammar school chums to her father's business associates had been sought out to attend. Agnes made sure of it.

But Sara thought little of the gala that was planned on her behalf. Many of those attending were selected because of the job prospects they may offer in the future. One, the president of a local college, had been pointed out to Sara many times. It was Helen's hope that Sara would bypass teaching the young, and instead focus on instructing college students while earning a masters degree. And if she should snag the wealthy son of a professor in the process, all the better.

Yes, it would be a big social event, just like so many Sara had attended while growing up. Only this one could have long-ranging career implications, if Sara decided to pursue them. The impression she made today could well determine the path her life would take.

Dropping to a chair, Sara grabbed a brush and briskly worked her way through her hair. Her elbow hit an envelope which fell to the ground. Reaching to pick it up, John Olson's name stood out.

"Isn't that too bad," she thought. "Probably the only decent person invited, and he won't be able to attend."

Sara couldn't deny her disappointment. Her experience in North Platte seemed so distant. Squeezing her eyes shut, she tried to remember John's face. But all she could come up with was a feeling. It was one of comfort, like that of a well-loved throw one could draw close on a cold, stormy night. But there was also a feeling of excitement, something new and untried waiting just over the horizon.

A part of Sara wanted to recapture that feeling. And the only way she knew how to do that was to reconnect with John Olson. But his quick refusal to her invitation created a barrage of uncertainty. Was he trying to get out of seeing her? Had she misread this man, and the friendship they seemed to share?

True, she didn't know much about a rancher's life. He could very well be telling the truth. Perhaps this was his busy season and he had no way of getting away. After all, she was in no position to judge his motives.

And what about his closing? It seemed so unlike John to use the word love, even in the innocence of a letter's farewell. He was such a quiet and reserved person. It seemed as if he carefully weighed each word before speaking. Wouldn't he use the same careful deliberation when writing a note — even a short note that said "no" loud and clear?

Fingering the letter, Sara angrily berated herself. "I really don't have the time to be thinking about this today. After all, it is supposed to be my day. Yet here I am, fretting over one when there will be so many others attending my party. Get over it, Sara."

Getting dressed, she tried to push the thought of John Olson out of her mind. By the time she slipped on her shoes, and shot a final approving glance in the mirror, she had almost succeeded.

The day went much as Sara expected it would. The graduation party went fine. A little boring, maybe, but fine none-the-less. After the usual speeches, Sara took her turn walking across the stage to receive her diploma. An immense sense of relief flooded her as she realized she'd done it — she'd accomplished her goal. Sitting down to watch the rest of the graduates, Sara began to mentally plot her next move.

It was ironic, actually. She had spent months worrying about this day. But no — that wasn't entirely true. It wasn't the graduation itself that had so occupied her as the transformation it would have on her life. The commencement ceremony had loomed like an enormous stopper in her future. Behind it were the choices and decisions life beyond college would demand. The sheepskin she held in her hand was a catalyst for the changes now possible in her life. The stopper was now removed, and Sara felt excitement rise nervously in her throat as her future's bittersweet nectar prepared to flow.

Sauntering into her graduation party later, Sara greeted the many guests enthusiastically. Her mother had hired an orchestra for the event, and as their tunes floated onto the dance floor Sara swayed gracefully in the arms of several different partners. Some of the guests who twirled her across the floor were slightly older than Sara—son's of businessmen Agnes saw fit to invite.

Dressed in stark white shirts framed by dark suits, Sara had to admit many of the guests looked handsome—even striking in their formal attire. Several of the young men were already making their marks. Some were following the wishes of their parents, but a few were following their own calling.

Those were the ones that interested Sara. She enjoyed hearing about their newest business adventure. They would talk in low voices that blended with the trumpet's nervous wine.

In a way, Sara was also turned off by their easy confidences. They felt safe discussing their business ventures with her. Too safe. After all, she was just a woman. What possible repercussions could there be in sharing a few secret details about their most recent business conquest?

As they spoke, Sara's face maintained an unguarded innocence that camouflaged her thoughts. One of her partners, big in shipping exports, reported nonchalantly that he was planning to buy a small New York carrier. At once Sara recognized the name. The company was owned by an elderly gentlemen by the name of Van Pelt. Her father had done business with him before. He had built his company from the ground up and was extremely proud of his accomplishment and his businesses good name. The old shipper had fought hard for the recognition his company was known for. With him, it wasn't just a business. It was his life.

While the tall, clean cut young man boasted about the offer he planned to present, Sara found it difficult to contain herself. Van Pelt would never sell to this young, inexperienced businessman. He would never risk the fruits from so many years of labor be squandered.

Yet, the young man went on, anxious to make himself look seasoned and capable in Sara's eyes. By the time the second dance was over, Sara gracefully begged off the dance floor. She had enough of her partner's transparent and inept manipulation.

Strolling outside for a breath of fresh air, Sara made her way to a second-floor balcony. High above, the stars twinkled down from their dark pillow of velvet. A light brush of wind cupped the scent of nearby lilac and tossed it about lavishly. The evening air carried a faint spring chill that tickled Sara's exposed back and chased a shiver up the base of her neck. Drawing her sheer, dusty blue shawl close, Sara leaned against the hard cement rail.

Did she feel the way she had imagined she would? No. So much of the anxiety she felt in the fall and winter had simply vanished.

She couldn't really explain her change of heart. Her fears and anxiety had simply drifted away, little by little, until all that was left was a deep-seeded feeling everything would somehow work out in the end. The trick, Sara decided, was being able to take it slowly — one step at a time — and enjoy the road to getting there.

This point had been driven home during her trip to Colorado. And, of course, her experience in Nebraska. Being forced to sit still long enough to listen and appreciate where she was had become part of the lesson.

Deep down, Sara knew a good deal of her attitude change could be traced back to a man called John Olson. His quiet yet determined manner steadied and calmed her even now, so many months after their meeting.

"It's too bad he couldn't make it. I wonder if he was telling the truth, or just making excuses to get out of coming," she thought.

She turned his note over in her mind, trying to understand what hidden meanings it might hold. His invitation to her had seemed honest enough. Should she take him up on it?

No. No, she wouldn't — couldn't. If his invitation wasn't sincere, she would feel like a fool.

Still, the time to make such a trip would be now. Very soon, she would have to make some type of career move. Her ambitious nature would not allow much time to pass. And so what if John couldn't make it to her graduation. After all, it seemed out of character for him to lie. He probably was as busy as he said.

"It's not like I know anything about ranching, after all," she muttered quietly.

With that, she made her way back to the celebration, dancing and laughing until the sun threatened to sweep the darkness away.

***

Several days later, Sara found herself in her father's study, the phone gripped tightly in her hand. After reading the numbers from a small slip of paper, she dialed quickly and brought the phone to her ear.

After a few minutes, the line crackled briefly and a woman's strong, sure voice rang out.

"Hello. This is the Olsons."

"Yes, I was wondering—wondering if John might be there," Sara said, speaking slowly.

"Oh! Well, yes. I think I saw him walk across the yard. Hang on a minute and let me check."

Sara heard a dull thud as the phone was set down. After a time, she could hear the thin sound of the woman calling John's name in the distance. The spring on a screen door screeched out.

"Hello, this is John." he said, his voice booming.

"Hello, stranger. What are you up to?"

"Sara? Sara! Good to hear from you! How was graduation?"

"Oh, you know. No big deal."

"Sorry I couldn't make it."

"That's O.K. I'll get even with you. Actually, that's why I'm calling. How would you like a visitor?"

"Your planning to come?"

"If I'm invited."

"Absolutely. Your absolutely invited. I'd like you to see Nebraska when it isn't buried under snow. And I'm sure dad would be happy to see you again, too."

Sara glanced at a calender on her father's desk.

"How does the second week in June look?"

"That would be good. How long will you be staying?"

"Maybe a week—two at the most."

"That should work out fine."

"Let's see... Could you give me the name of a hotel in town? I don't think the hospital will be taking reservations this time of year."

John smiled silently at the joke.

"Don't worry about that. We've got plenty of room here at the ranch." John shot a look across the room at his mother, who had been listening to the conversation with eyes widened. "I'm sure mom wouldn't have it any other way," he added, shooting a grin across the room.

"Well... I guess. If you're sure it won't be a problem."

"Good. Then it's settled."

"Good. I'll drop you a note after I finalize arrangements."

"I'll be looking forward to it."

As he hung up the phone, John's smile slipped from his face. His mother watched in interest as the look of joy on his face dissolved into one of horror.

"Oh my God! What am I going to do!? How am I going to keep a high-caliber New York girl like Sara Morris entertained? She'll be bored in an hour!"

Helen's shoulders began to bounce up and down uncontrollably as laughter welled in her throat. She dabbed lightly at the corners of her eyes with an apron.

"John Olson. I have never seen you so rattled. This girl must really be something!"

Helen laughed for a few more seconds before getting a hold of herself.

"Don't worry, John. I'm sure she wouldn't be coming all the way back out here if she hadn't been impressed the first time. And besides, we are what we are. It's a little late in the game to try changing now."

Still flustered, John walked outside. He knew there was something pressing he needed to do, but he couldn't remember what it was. He ended up walking to the corral, staring off blankly into the distance.

"For heavens sake. Grab hold of yourself, you dummy," he thought while standing at the corral gate, deeply lost in thought.

In spite of her initial ambivalence, Sara was actually looking forward to her Nebraska trip anxiously. After so many months of being tied down to college, it felt good to be on the move—without any serious obligations. The whole thing was like a big adventure and Sara was ready to embrace it wholeheartedly.

And nature seemed to be in full support of her feelings. The day she was to leave the sun showed down brightly, teasing the grass and trees into a deep green blush. Birds threw their songs up to the heavens, carefree.

Sara had made a point of picking an outfit that fit her optimistic mood. She had grabbed a white satin number out of her closet. The dress had capped sleeves and was dotted with hundreds of blooming red roses. To top things off, she'd grabbed a large white hat that held a length of tulle atop the brim. Gazing in her closet, she'd briefly debated between wearing a white pair of pumps or a shiny red ones that exactly matched the color of roses on her dress.

After only a moments hesitation, the red shoes were upon her feet. And Sara was out the door, headed for a new adventure.

The train trip seemed to go along more quickly than it had on her first journey. Acre after acre of green pastures slipped by her window. Every so often, the train would slow as it went through a town, or stop completely. When it did, she took pleasure in watching children jumping rope or playing jacks in front yards.

Usually, the train would pass by the huge silos of small-town grain co-ops. Men in overalls and dusty caps would be propped around a pickup or gathered in small groups. They looked like they were hashing things over—maybe the latest prices, or even the latest gossip. Sara couldn't tell, from her distant perch. But there was no misunderstanding the easy, familiar manner in which these men stood around exchanging their banter.

Watching them, so alike from town to town, gave Sara a sense of familiarity. Like a framed work of art hanging on a gallery wall, she could imagine herself stepping into their world and becoming a part of it. She would imagine the group full of familiar faces, people she had grown up with and known throughout her life. She would know their wives, children and grand children. What they were loved for and what they had done to be despised.

But then reality would set in and she would realize the pictures were places she could not enter — things to which she did not belong to. Slowly, the train would pull away, propelling Sara back into her own life. And like so many soft oils, the scenery would flip by with scenes more frequent than she could absorb or understand.

Lost in thought, Sara reflected on what was drawing her ever westward to a place where she had no connection, no ties to speak of. By all accounts, it was completely unreasonable. Her mother had told her so several times before leaving. Would her time have been better spent staying around New York and looking for a job?

No, judging from her negative feelings, that would have been a mistake. Sara felt like she was already carrying around a lot of unnecessary baggage. She had to get rid of it before moving on. And in order to do that, it was necessary to get away from her mother's influence and think for herself for awhile.

Sara's brow furrowed deeply. Was that what she was doing? Was she running away? The revelation didn't appeal to her. She'd always considered herself a strong person. One who was willing to do whatever it took to get where she wanted to go. The idea of running to Nebraska and cowering from her mother's influence made Sara bristle in anger.

But while it may be part of the reason for Sara's trip, she knew it wasn't the only one. Mile after mile, she pondered what the other reasons may be. But it seemed as though just when she was about to get the answer, the genie would again disappear into his bottle, maddeningly keeping his secret.

Of one thing Sara was sure. The whole thing was an adventure. It gave her a feeling of independence that she savored over and over again. Going to Nebraska was an idea none of her friends would have entertained. It seemed wild and adventuresome—an experience that would be hers alone.

And what was John Olson's role in all this? Again, Sara had no clear answers. From the moment she met him, he had been a friend. Someone who was willing to share of himself but also able to stop and listen. He seemed interested in hearing what Sara had to say.

His efforts to listen weren't the self-absorbed attempts to humor her she'd seen other men try to use. But John seemed open to new ideas. Like places he'd never been, he was willing to explore Sara's thoughts without criticism or preconceived notions.

At last, the train pulled into the North Platte station. Sara was more than ready to leave, the monotonous journey and her revolving thoughts wearing on her mind. Stepping out of the car, a brisk prairie wind pushed against her legs. Holding a small bag with one hand, she made her way down a boarding platform made of old railroad ties. Her bright red shoes twisted from side to side as they disappeared between large, jagged pieces of white crushed rock.

Just as she was about to stumble, a strong hand clutched her elbow. Peering up from beneath her large-brimmed hat, she recognized her old friend.

"My, look what the wind blew in," John said, his eyes crinkled with laughter.

"Did you save all this up for me? I swear, winter or spring, you can count on Nebraska to deal a nasty hand," Sara said as John helped her into his car.

Once the car door was shut, Sara breathed a sigh of relief. John disappeared behind the train depot and returned a short time later with Sara's luggage in hand. After popping them into the trunk, he moved to open the car door. Another sudden blast of wind shot through the vehicle, blowing Sara's hat to the floor and tossing her hair about frantically.

As John slid into the car and slammed his door closed, the two eyed each other.

"Did you order up this weather especially for my arrival?," Sara said, picking her hat up off the floor and dusting it off.

John smiled as he slid the key into the ignition and turned it sharply. Donning a lame southern drawl he bantered good-naturedly.

"Why, this ain't nothin', ma'am. You ought to see our snow storms."

The trusty old green car turned towards the ranch.

Everywhere Sara looked, the trees and grass strained against the winds persistent wrath. Despite the weather's tiring presence, Sara was pleased with what she saw. Before and after the winter's raging blizzard the land had seemed barren and forbidding—a no man's land without mercy for those unfortunate enough to call it home.

But the green flowing grassland seemed to deny such a time had existed. Everywhere she looked, a celebration of life was underway. As the cattle grazed lazily beyond neat rows of fence, they seemed unconcerned, even bored with the favors nature had so generously granted.

Sara and John made idle small talk. John clutched the steering wheel tightly. He had calmed most of his initial fears about keeping his guest entertained for two weeks. But seeing her tugged at his insecurities, giving them rise once again. With difficulty, he was managing to keep his feelings in check. And even though the young New Yorker at his side was causing him such anxiety, he did feel himself slipping into the sense of familiarity they enjoyed in snow storms midst.

As they pulled into John's driveway, Sara gasped in surprise. Cars were parked crowded onto the yard with a few spilling over into a nearby field.

"Surprise," John said, noting her reaction. "We invited a few friends over to help welcome you back to Nebraska."

As John and Sara entered the Olson house, she was greeted by a crowd of people seated on couches and visiting in circles. Helen had seen their car pull up and was immediately by Sara's side.

"Well hello, there, dear. It's so nice you could make it back to visit. I've heard so much about what you were put through by my two men during the storm. What a brave girl you must be, coming back here after all that."

Ed squeezed his way through the guests and took Sara's hand in his.

"Why, look at what the wind blew in. I can't believe you made it back. It's good to have you." Drawing Sara closer, he lowered his voice. "Now, listen, the women are going to talk your arm off but don't you let 'em. I'm sure your hungry after your trip and we've got food. And lots of it. So if you'll lead the way, we'll get this show on the road."

A makeshift buffet had been set up on the dining room table. As Helen set a large piece of barbecued beef on the table, everyone snapped into motion. Sara was handed a plate and began serving herself as others followed. She was then shown to a seat on the couch.

Before long, everyone had a plate of savory meat, vegetables and all the fixings. In between bites, Sara was introduced to some of the people attending. The group peppered her with questions about her family and trip to Nebraska.

After eating, the men disappeared into the garage, where tables had been set up to play cards. The women milled around, picking up dishes and exchanging the latest news.

Sara was amazed at how friendly everyone appeared to be. She slipped into a friendly discussion with those present, just as she had with John. *I*

"It must just be the nature of these people, to accept others without questioning," she thought. Of one thing she was sure—the people at home would never be so open to a stranger.

Several hours later, after a series of handshakes and cheerful farewells, the last guests left. The women attending had cleaned up most of the mess from the party and the house looked almost as if nothing had ever happened.

John and Sara made their way out to the porch. The wind had quieted with the falling sun, leaving only a mild breeze.

"Sorry about that," John said. "I guess I should have warned you the welcoming committee would be here. It was my parents idea. I hope it wasn't too much."

"Oh, no. It was nice, actually. I'm glad they did it."

A few clouds snaked across the moon giving them a silver glow. Sara sighed quietly.

"Well, I'll bet you're tired. Mom's got a room upstairs ready for you."

The two trailed into the house, the old screen door squeaking a yawn as they entered. Helen showed Sara to her room. Within minutes of undressing, Sara fell into the soft feather pillow and drifted into a sound sleep.

She awoke early the next morning to the sound of an engine revving. Looking out her window she saw an old truck backing towards a loading chute beside the corral. After two tries, the driver was apparently satisfied with his location. As the ignition was shut off, the old truck hiccuped and backfired loudly.

Throwing open a suitcase, Sara rummaged through until she found a pair of jeans, cotton shirt and soft Angora sweater. A few minutes later, she was downstairs.

"Good morning," Helen said as she flipped a sizzling sausage over in the skillet. "Looks like the old truck got you up."

"Yes, good morning. What is going on?"

"It's sale day," John said, striding through the room and grabbing a piece of toast from the table. "And guess whose invited?"

After eating a quick breakfast, Helen shooed Sara outside to watch the cattle be loaded. Zeke and Ed were in the pen sorting the animals. Ed stood off to the side, eyeing them closely. His leather-gloved hands rested on a sturdy old stick and every so often he would single out a cow with the wave of a finger. Shouting "Yep, Yep," John and Zeke would isolate the calf and chase it into a side pen. When the trio was satisfied calves too small were held back, the rest were herded into the big old truck.

John, Sara and Ed crawled into the cab and headed out the driveway for the sale barn. The ride was bumpy, and dirt got into the poorly-sealed cab. Sara sneezed a few times as clouds if dust filled the air.

When they reached the North Platte sale barn, John repeated the backing process. As the calves were unloaded, a barn employee jotted down the number of cattle delivered and escorted them into a pen to await the auction.

The trio made their way into the sale barn. By then, the arena was quite full. A few order buyers sat just outside the ring. Every so often the auctioneer would announce one of the specialty buyers had a phone call. They would make their way to a small ringside enclosure that was equipped with a phone.

Sara watched the same scene unfold over and over again. One of the men in the sale ring would lazily pull a large gate open. John whispered to Sara the ring helpers were called field men. A group of young cows would crowd into the ring and mill around in circles while an auctioneer got bids from farmers and ranchers.

A sour smell wafted through the high-topped, circular sale ring area. Persistent flies clung to the beasts body's and swarmed annoyingly around around the faces of those who watched. Sara watched as several men at the auction chomped down absentmindedly on hamburgers brought in from the sale barn cafe.

"Yep. Yep. Yep," the auctioneer shouted again and again as he went back and forth between bidders. His voice was smooth and continual, a steady stream of babble that was musical but held no meaning for Sara. Eventually, the cows would be sold and another gate, this one on the far end of the ring, would swing open. The cattle would prance out, and the whole process would begin again.

Finally, Sara could no longer contain herself. The process going on in front of her was unlike anything she'd learned in business school. Leaning towards John, she whispered, "How can these people sell and buy cattle without a written contract?"

Smiling, John said, "A man's word or hand shake is our contract."

Sara's puzzlement disappeared as the herdsman threw open the gate and quickly ran for the sale ring fence. With a flurry of dust, an enormous bull charged into the open area. It's dark coat was matched by the silent fury in eyes. Frantically, the frothing beast kicked up its back hooves and lowered its horned head menacingly. Sara noticed one of the warriors pointed weapons was shorter but rubbed smooth from the passage of time.

The crowd hushed as the beasts musky odor wafted through the air. Lowering it's head, the bull charged towards the elevated auctioneers booth. The sound of cracking wood resonated through the building.

Frustrated and even more outraged, the animal swung its flanks around and set its sights beyond the sale ring fence. Sara's interest turned to horror as the angry beast seemed to glower at her as it snorted a fierce warning. The auctioneers voice halted and the onlookers fell into silence.

Sara sat frozen, hypnotized by the hatred pulsing throughout the bull's body. She felt a persistent tug as John cupped her arm and gently guided her away from their ringside seat. As she moved back, Sara kept her eyes on the bull, watching as its tail twitched from side to side in defiance.

In a single, fluid motion the bull lurched forward. Raising it's front hooves off the ground, the massive animal looked, for a brief second, like a trained circus dog performing a trite routine. Raising its front hooves 10-feet off the ground, the bull seemed to be floating through the air. But the illusion quickly disappeared as its weighty legs slapped down on the sale-ring fence.

Teetering across the top bar, the onlookers gasped as the bull's head and shoulders lurched forward. It's massive horns were just inches away from where Sara sat moments before. With back legs floundering, the animal kicked wildly like a child's marionette. Snorts burst from its nostrils shooting a fine mist of sweat into the air.

The black devil hung there for a moment, its front hooves perilously close to reaching the freedom. With a sudden burst of energy, the bull gave one final kick, his hooves gashing the ring's wooden frame. Unable to find firm footing, it panicked and slipped backwards. As one hoof hit the ground, the brute lost it's balance and fell hard on its side.

Like a fish plucked from water, the bull flopped on the ground. Rolling in soft green manure, it flailed frantically. A herdsman reached into the ring and flipped open the exit door. The infuriated animal achingly found its feet. Spotting the open door, it loped through, throwing its head from side to side as it rounded the corner.

Sara tried to digest the scene which had just taken place. It was beyond anything she had ever witnessed. The genteel passiveness of her New York friends flashed through her mind.

"I'd like to see a bull like that on the golf course," she thought.

Sara and John looked at each other, sighing in relief.

"Maybe we'd better call it a day," John said.

"I think that would be a good idea," Sara answered.

The next day, John asked Sara if she would like to drive down to meet the Olson's neighbors. Sara quickly agreed and on the way there, John filled her in. Greg and Mary Lou Henn were a young couple who had grown up in the area. Their acreage was located on a corner of the Henn ranch, which was owned by Gregg's parents. The couple owned a good-sized herd of cattle. Gregg also helped his parents with their herd.

As John and Sara pulled into the driveway, Gregg and Mary Lou were just getting into their pickup. Sara noted it looked like a newer-model truck, perhaps a sign the couple was doing well.

Seeing John's pickup pull in, Gregg got out of the cab and slammed the door.

"I hope you're not coming here to tell me I've got cattle out," Gregg said, smiling as he drew near.

"Nope. Looks like you're safe this time, at least. Gregg, I've got somebody here I'd like you to meet. This is Sara Morris. She's come from New York to see what ranching is all about."

"It's a pleasure to meet you," Gregg said, extending his hand past John. "Yep, if you've been here a while, you already know cattle can be hard. Like they say in that John Wayne movie, they're just a lot of trouble wrapped up in a leather bag."

"It looks like we caught you at a bad time. Thought we'd come over for a little visit," John said.

"Have them come with us," Mary Lou shouted from the pickup cab. "I packed enough for an army."

"We were just headed up to the meadow for a little picnic dinner. Would you like to come?," Gregg said.

"Well, that's O.K. We can come back later. We didn't mean to impose."

"Hell, that ain't no imposition. Mary Lou always packs too much anyway. Like I need it. Besides, it would give your guest a chance to see the real Nebraska. We can't have Miss Morris going back to New York with noth'in but a post-card image of your cattle herd in her head."

John nodded, laughing. Before long the two trucks were following each other through a bumpy pasture. As they approached a grove of trees, the ground smoothed into a green carpet of grass. Passing through a narrow clearing, Sara gasped in surprise. Stretching wide was the softly flowing water of the Platte River.

Mary Lou tossed a blanket out on the soft grass. Sara got out of the pickup to help and quickly struck up a conversation with the rancher's wife.

"My, I didn't realize we were so close to the river. It's really beautiful," Sara said watching the sun dance playfully atop the gently rippling water.

Setting down a picnic basket, Mary Lou absentmindedly pushed a strand of hair behind her ear.

"Yes, I guess it is, in a way. When you live by it your whole life, it just gets to be something your used to. We kind of take it for granted. Do you have any place like this in New York?"

Sara laughed as she sat down. "Not hardly. Everything in New York is surrounded by concrete — and people. Lots of people. There's never really a place to go where you can count on being alone. And if you are, it's time to worry."

Gregg and John came near toting along a few fishing poles and a bucket of bait. They set their poles down a few feet downstream and set to work getting the supplies organized. With a flip of his wrist Gregg sent a weight and bobber flying through the air. A few feet away, John did the same. After a few more casts the pair was satisfied. Propping up their poles, the two made their way towards the blanket.

80

A large plastic filled with fried chicken appeared, followed by a tub of mashed potatoes and gravy. Mary Lou also produced a plate of freshly-baked rolls and a still-warm cherry pie.

Gregg wasted no time digging into the meal. Sara initially hesitated, but after taking a bite of the fried chicken she was certain she had never tasted anything so delicious.

"My, this is wonderful," Sara said as she reached for another piece. "What in the world did you do to make this chicken taste so wonderful."

Mary Lou pressed her lips together to control her smile. "Maybe it tastes so good to you because it's fresh. I dressed it this morning."

Sara eyed the leg in her fingers suspiciously. A few hours earlier, her dinner had been strutting across the yard, without so much as a care. Now it was on her plate. Sara had never had qualms about eating meat before, but she had never been aware of the process that got it to her plate.

"So, do you two come down here often?," Sara said, inconspicuously slipping her plate behind the picnic basket.

"Oh, we try to, when we can," Mary Lou said, cutting into the pie. "It's nice for a change. And if we're lucky, Gregg catches a little something for supper."

Sara graciously accepted the pie offered to her, savoring each mouthful. After the dishes were cleared and tucked back into the picnic basket, Sara and Mary Lou sat on the blanket, legs outstretched facing the river.

Across the water, a muddy bank fought to keep in the water's flow. Above it, a rocky cliff jutted out. Sara was amazed that such a dramatic geological contrast could take place in such a small area. And it was significantly different compared to the New York scenery she had grown up with.

"It's amazing how much variety there is in the United States. And the difference in people is even more dramatic. Everyone seems to be in their own little tribe. And once in, it's so difficult to ever see beyond," Sara thought.

"So, Sara, what is it that you do?," Mary Lou asked.

"Actually, I just graduated from college. I'm not quite sure what direction I'll be taking."

"Really. What did you get a degree in?"

"Teaching. And business. But teaching is first."

81

"I see," Mary Lou said, glancing at Sara. "Interesting. You know, there's a position open at the grade school. Mrs. Leggot finally retired. She was old when she taught me. Maybe you could check it out. You know, kind of see what a Nebraska school can offer."

Sara looked squarely at Mary Lou. Raising her brows, she turned her gaze back to the river.

A short time later, Gregg and John returned carrying a five-gallon bucket. Five catfish milled around nervously in their small enclosure.

"Looks like we've used up our luck for one day," Gregg said. "Just as well get back and take care of these.

The group prepared to go their separate ways. Before leaving, Sara shot a final glance across her shoulder at the lumbering Platte.

Back at the Olson's, John left to do chores while Sara headed for her room. The river's lazy lull made Sara relaxed and drowsy. Before drifting off to sleep, she thought about the Henn's down-to-earth attitude. Their life seemed so simple. Even life and death ebbed and blended into their lives unquestioned. It was a part of an ongoing cycle her New York counterparts had cut themselves off from; a part themselves they denied knowledge of.

The sound of the flowing river came back to Sara, carrying her to sleep.

At breakfast the next morning, John told Sara he would need to spend the day working cattle.

"If you'd like, you could use the car to drive into North Platte and see if town has anything to offer," John said.

"You mean there's more there than a hospital lobby?," Sara said, laughing.

"Well, maybe not much more. Anyway, the keys are hanging by the door, if you would like to go. We will be working the cattle right here on the yard if you need anything."

After John left, Sara considered her options. Drumming her fingers across the table-top, she spotted a phone book sitting atop the kitchen counter. Flipping through it, she found the number for the North Platte Elementary School.

A short time later, she was heading into town. As the car traveled down the bumpy road, Sara silently berated herself.

"This is crazy. I know it. But what the heck. At least I'll be better prepared for my next interview," she thought.

Sara made her way over the railroad tracks that had brought her west so many times. A few blocks later, the old hospital came into view and with it, a flood of memories.

Before she knew it, she was sitting in front of an old, two-story brick building. Above the front door, a concrete archway displayed the boldly etched words: North Platte Grade School — 1920.

She visited with the principal, Mr. Murdock briefly, indicating she was visiting a friend in the area and had just learned about the teaching position. After what Sarah thought was a productive interview, Mr. Murdock gave Sara a tour of the building and the classroom in need of a teacher.

Before leaving, Sara couldn't help but be impressed. Although far from any cultural centers, it appeared to her the North Platte people put much stock in their young people. She promised to mail her full resume to Mr. Murdock after returning to New York.

Then, Sara found downtown North Platte and wandered into one of the shops. She was a little disappointed with the selection. It was just a fraction of what a New York boutique would offer, and most of it was pitifully out of style. But she was amused with the small store's novelty and spent several hours going from shop to shop.

For lunch, she stopped at a small corner diner. Sunlight streamed in and made the highly-polished beige-tile floor gleam. Sara made her way to the counter where she sat on a red-plastic stool. A woman in a starched pink dress that exactly matched the color of her lipstick handed her a menu.

"Hello, honey. We've got anything on the menu and our dinner special is right there," she said, motioning to a chalk board propped up beside the serving window. Pulling a pencil from behind her ear, she licked the tip and poised it atop a small order pad. "What can I start you off with today?"

"Oh, I'll just get the soup. And a glass of iced tea."

"Eat'in kind'a light today, aren't ya, honey?"

Sara cracked a smile. In a place where everyone was acquainted, it should have come as no shock that a complete stranger would be worried about her eating habits.

"I had a big breakfast."

"Have it your way, honey." Ripping a sheet off the order form, the pink-lipped woman pivoted around, stuck the paper in an order carousel and shouted, "Order. Get with the program, speedy."

The cafe became increasingly crowded. People from all walks of life began drifting in. At a corner booth, Sara saw a group of men in suits congregated — no doubt from the bank across the street. Several men in blue-denim overall gathered in the center of the cafe, exchanging information on the latest crop and livestock prices. Their cigarette smoke scented the air and hung over the room. A few families drifted in, harried mothers and helpful fathers ready to rest after a morning of shopping.

When Sara received the warm, home-made soup, she quickly drained the bowl. She left a sizable tip, and ventured back into the street to finish taking in the downtown area.

By the time she arrived home, it was nearing 5 p.m. As she slowly guided the car in the Olson's garage, John came out to meet her.

"My, I didn't know there was that much to do in North Platte."

"There isn't. But that didn't stop me," Sara said, removing a few small packages from the back seat.

"Well, time to get ready. We're headed for the rodeo tonight."

"Didn't you get enough of that at the sale barn?"

"Oh, that was just a taste of the excitement you'll witness this evening."

"O.K., I guess I'll get ready," Sara said, slipping into the house.

The evening was calm and balmy. John and Sara entered the noisy outdoor arena and squeezed into a spot on the bleachers. The event was already in progress, and they arrived just in time to see a rodeo clown racing away from an angry bull. Sara gasped as the clown jumped into a rubber barrel just as the bull bumped it with his head.

"A friend of mine is going to be riding tonight. I thought it might be nice to cheer him on," John said.

Time after time, eager riders would take their chances atop the rowdy bulls. The eight seconds they needed to complete a ride seemed to go on forever and few were able to make the cut.

Finally, John's friend lowered himself into the pen for a chance to win. As the doors flew open, the bull began swinging around in a circle, kicking madly. For a few seconds, it appeared the rider would win the battle. But John and Sara watched in horror as he was suddenly toppled to one side.

Within a second, the rider was thrown from the bull, but his hand remained caught in the rope handle. Pulled like a rag doll, the man's body went limp as it was yanked from side to side.

As the eight-second buzzer sounded, two clowns leapt out to distract the bull, motioning frantically to divert the beasts attention. But he would have none of it. The bull's rear leg came down hard on its captives free arm.

Finally, the rider slipped from his deathly tourniquet and the bull sped to the far side of the arena. Amazingly, the man got up, but held his arm gingerly as he left the arena.

Sara's mouth pursed. "What in the world is wrong with these people? Are they completely suicidal?," she thought.

Eventually, the final buzzer sounded and John and Sara headed home.

"Well, what did you think?" John asked.

"I thought those riders were insane. What could they be thinking?"

"It's a difficult and challenging sport, that's true. But most of those people are around cattle all the time. It's just a part of life for them."

"Not that they'll have much life to worry about. It just doesn't seem worth it to me."

"I guess it just depends on who you ask," John said.

By then, it was late. John's parents had left the porch light on, and the old screen door squeaked loudly as the two entered the house.

"That was quite a bit of excitement for one night. I'll be happy to turn in," Sara said.

"I've had it, too. Better get some rest. We've got something different planned for you tomorrow," John said.

When Sara made it downstairs the next morning, she was greeted by several flatbed trailers lined outside. Helen was filling a large cooler with lemonade and told Sara it was time to bail hay.

John crawled atop a cheery-red Farmall "M" tractor and Sara hopped up on the flatbed behind it. Slowly, he made his way down the road to a hay field about two miles away. Ed followed with a bailer and another flatbed. Zeke and Helen took up the rear, riding in a pickup hitched to two more flatbeds.

At the field, a number of young, high school-aged boys were ready and waiting for the day's work to begin. John pulled his tractor off to the side. When Ed reached the field, the young men headed for the flatbed.

John let down the bail chute at the rear of the machine and adjusted the twine tension. With a lurch he started down an alfalfa row Zeke had mowed and raked a few days earlier.

Rickety-clack, rickety-clack, rickety-clack, the bailer sang as it scooped the row of alfalfa into its gaping auger-mouth. The alfalfa was gradually packed into a hay bail that slowly made its way out the back of the machine. One of the young men then reached down to pluck it up, throwing it neatly in place atop the rack.

For a while, Sara rode along on the hay rack. The alfalfa smelled green and sweet, but its stems were sharp to the touch. Occasional gusts of wind blew dried alfalfa leaves into her face and hair. When space got tight on the rack, she jumped off and went to sit in the truck with Mrs. Olson.

"Well, what do you think of today?," Helen asked.

"It's a lot of work, that's for sure. Will the cattle eat all this over the winter?"

"This and much more. We should get at least two more cuttings. Three if it rains. Last winter, we needed every bit of it, especially since the snow covered up all the grass and there was nothing else for the cattle to eat."

"That's amazing. The biggest thing I'm used to feeding is a dog," Sara said.

The two sat there in silence for a few minutes, watching the trailer fill up. When the last bail was fitted on, the flatbed was pulled to the far corner of the field. There, a second group was busy unloading the bails and creating one enormous hay stack.

Ed had taken over driving the tractor, and John had moved to helping the crew atop the stack. Sara watched in interest as John tossed the heavy bails effortlessly.

"He's really something. Works like a horse but has one of the best hearts I've ever seen. It was so nice of him to give me this opportunity. I would have never realized there was anything but the New York way of life if I hadn't come out here. I'm sure I'll remember this experience for the rest of my life," Sara thought.

As lunch neared, Helen and Sara went home to whip up something to eat. They returned with pork sandwiches, chips, iced tea and still-warm home-made apple pie. Helen spread the food out on the open pickup gate and the crew began drawing near. In no time, the food they brought was completely cleaned up.

Sara enjoyed the meal, seasoned with the fields sweet perfume and sky's limitless generosity. As the men made small-talk between bites, a solitary meadow lark provided a symphony of background music.

After the men were done eating and returned to work, John lagged behind. He joined Sara as she casually leaned against the pickup box.

"So, what do you think? It's not exactly a trip to the museum," John said.

"But more fun. I really have to thank you, John."

"For what? Putting you to work?"

"No, silly. Putting up with me like this. There's a lot of work out here I never imagined. I have to confess, it crossed my mind that you were just making excuses not to attend my college graduation. But now I can see you were being honest."

"Yes, there's something to keep a person busy out here all year around. But there are advantages — at least that's what I hear. When you learn what they are, you can let me know," John said, smirking.

"Oh, stop it. You've been in New York and know how different it is. No crowds, no rude people, lots of space. You know, you're right. I just don't know how you can stand it," Sara said, nudging John with her elbow playfully.

"Ha! Well, looks like I'd better get back at it. Can't have our hired help goofing off."

Sara and Helen stuck around to see the tractor make two more rounds and then headed home. After the two finished cleaning up the kitchen, Sara asked if she could use the telephone. Helen agreed, leaving the room to do some sewing.

"Well, I just as well get this over with," Sara muttered, quickly dialing her home telephone number and listened impatiently as it rang.

"Hello, this is the Morris residence." It was the voice of Merle, the family butler.

"Hi, Merle, it's Sara. Is dad around?"

"Ah, Miss. Morris. So good to hear from you. I'm sorry, but your father has left for the afternoon.

Signing, Sara rolled her eyes. "Well, I'm probably going to regret asking this, but is mother there?"

"I believe you are in luck, Miss Morris. Let me see if I can locate her."

The telephone thumped lightly as it was laid down. Sara listened intently to the vacant silence on the other end of the line. She would have thought the phone was disconnected had it not been for the distant, gentle ticking of the old grandfather clock in the hallway.

The seconds trudged by. Sara was not looking forward to this conversation. Her mother had been against her trip to Nebraska from the start. It was Agnes' contention her daughter's time would have better spent attending teas at the bridge club or making herself available to young bachelors at evening socials.

"I wonder what she'd do if I got interested in Fred Baxter. After all, his dad is a powerful attorney. Too bad he couldn't file an injunction against his son picking his nose. You'd think a man in his 20's would have outgrown such a disgusting habit," Sara thought.

Sara was ripped from her thought by the sound of the phone being picked up.

"Sara, darling. What in the world have you been up to? I thought the Indians had most surely done away with you."

"Mother, that isn't funny. I just called to check in. How's everything there?"

"Well. We're doing well. Your father landed a big job that's been keeping him distracted. Of course, I am doing fine. Well, I was, at least, until I found out that cad Mildred Wibblecraft had been invited to the scrabble tournament at the club. Can you believe it? Mildred Wibblecraft! Hidden Valley just isn't what it used to be."

"I'm sure you'll recover."

"And, dear, how are you? Are these people aware of who they have visiting them? Are they treating you with the respect a person of your caliber is entitled to, dear?"

"Yes, mother. They're very nice people. Look, I hate to cut this short, but I really do need to go. Please let dad know everything is going well, and I'll be heading home in about ten days."

"Very good. It will be nice to have you back where you belong."

"Goodbye, Mother."

Sara set down the receiver in relief.

"That could have gone a lot worse. I'm surprised she didn't demand I catch the next train home," Sara thought.

Left to her own devices, Sara wandered outside and ventured toward an old shed. Bracing against a sliding door, she pushed until it gave way to the building's dark interior. The gloomy building's old walls were lined with cob webs and a great number of antique tools. Some old farming equipment was tucked away into the corners, left to age in private dignity.

She made her way around the tool shed slowly, leaving a trail of dusty footprints while studying the building's treasures.Someone had made a nut and bolt caddy of old baby food jars. Rows of lids were nailed down to a horizontal, rotating dolly and mounted onto a caddy. As it was turned, the bolts struck against the glass bottles, playing a harsh, uneven melody.

Beneath a workbench that held an old electric grinder and vice grip, Sara spotted a rusted form that was once used to repair shoes. Running her hand across it's coarse frame the New Yorker felt herself being transported back to a distant time in Nebraska's past, where being self-sufficient was imperative. She tried to imagine being completely responsible for everything needed for survival — clothes, food and shelter, without the aid of other people.

"What a lonely life it must have been," Sara said, sighing.

Standing propped in an old whiskey barrel, an abandon scythe stood guard over years of forgotten labor and laborers. Behind it hung a hardened pair of leather gloves that still bore the shape of the hands they protected.

An old, steel toolbox was tucked firmly below the workbench, and Sara braced as she pulled backwards on its old wooden handle. Throwing up the work boxes heavy lid, a treasure-chest of tools was revealed. Lifting out the first layer, Sara peered into the boxes cavernous interior.

Inside she was surprised to see a carefully-wrapped length of light-brown fabric. Carefully lifting it out, she realized the parcel was covered with a layer of dust. Tapping the material gently, her hand struck a hard object held within. Sara slowly unwound the cloth, watching in interest as the coarse cotton material turned lighter and lighter shades until it held a faint white blush.

The material's final layer revealed a small, tattered book. It's tan cover was decorated with flowering scrolls except for one small, rectangular spot. On the smooth brown leather surface was a faded signature. Walking to a sunlit window, Sara took a deep breath and brushed the cover lightly. Straining, she made out the name Ole Blyhovde Olson.

Sara drifted out of the old shed and sat down on a worn stump used as a makeshift chair. With her back rested against the building, she flipped through the thin, brittle pages. After a few seconds, she realized the book in her hand was a diary that began on September 5, 1877. The first entry was written as Ole and his wife, Hanna, set sail from northern Europe.

As Sara flipped through the diary, she followed their trip as it progressed over the Atlantic Ocean. Through Ole Olson's eyes the fear and anticipation of what lie ahead came alive once again, decades after it was first penned.

Sara was transported back in time as rough ocean waters made the author's hand shake in fear. Sea-sickness and bouts of various illnesses were broken only by infrequent meals that consisted of dried bread.

As the ship sailed on, the author was given to bouts of despair. Questions about whether going to America was a wise decision continued to burden Ole's mind. Would America provide the type opportunities promised? Was leaving family and friends in Norway the best decision? Sara read of a man who was torn between the yearning of his heart and the need to find a better life.

After landing on the east coast, Sara followed the Olson's journey across the United States. They made their way to Wisconsin where they found work on a farm.

As Sara read the final page in the worn diary, the Ole Blyhovde Olson family had finally found a place to call home. It was in the barren, lonely state of Nebraska that they finally settled. A place those traveling through came to know as the sandhills.

Gingerly closing the diary, Sara's eyes drifted towards the horizon. She tried to imagine Ole and his family, seeing the land they were to call home for the first time. What they saw undoubtedly looked much the same, nature standing in defiance of man's plaintive efforts at change.

With her legs working on their own, Sara found herself drifting towards the house, the diary still clutched in her hand. Entering, she sat down at the kitchen table while Helen rattled dishes in the sink.

"Helen, who is Ole Blyhovde Olson?"

"Hummm. Let me think a minute. Why, that was Ed's great-great grandfather. He was one of the original settlers in this area. What makes you ask?"

"Well, I was looking through some things in the tool shed, and came across this," Sara said, holding the diary out in her hand.

Helen dried off her hands and moved to the table. As she took the diary in one hand, she used the other to slide out a chair and sit down. Adjusting her glasses, Helen strained to make out the writing on the cover as Sara had. After flipping through a few pages, Helen shook her head in wonder.

"Where in the world did you find this?," Helen said.

"In an old tool box."

"I can't believe it. I've certainly never seen this and I doubt that Ed did, either. It must have been out there for years. It's a wonder it wasn't accidentally destroyed."

"I've read it all the way through. It looks like a first-hand account of their trip to the United States."

Helen sat quietly, reading a few more pages. Sighing, she closed the book and set it down on the table.

"I think you've discovered a long-lost piece of our family history. I'm sure Ed and John will get a lot of enjoyment out of reading through this."

"I guess I didn't realize the history of John's ancestors. The Olson family roots run deep. It was a struggle to get here. But once they did, they stuck it out—for generations."

"That's right. It wasn't always easy for them. And there are still challenges. But being out here grows on a person. There's a freedom to it many people don't ever get to experience. Sometimes, we take it for granted. But now, thanks to you—and Ole, we'll all get a reminder of the struggle it really was."

For a moment, Sara and Helen were silent. Each was alone in their thoughts, contemplating a man who lived decades ago. A man who had taken a chance and in the process altered the lives of those who followed.

The silence was broken by the sudden crack of the screen door.

"Well, looks like we've got her licked for the day," Ed said, heading for the refrigerator to get a glass of iced tea. "John and Zeke are bringing the empty flatbeds home now."

Helen waved the diary at Ed.

"Looks like Sara came across something you've managed to miss all these years. Said she found this diary in an old tool box in the shed out back."

Ed rubbed a dusty hand on his overalls before taking the aged book.

"Well I'll be darned," he said in amazement, turning the book slowly. "I'll be darned."

***

Early the next day, the Olson's were ready to move cattle from one pasture to another. They set things up much as they did when moving the animals before the big snow storm. Sara and Helen took up positions along a county road to ensure they continued along straight and didn't wander in a different direction.

It took the animals a long time to arrive since it was necessary for John and Zeke to round them up on horseback. Finally, Sara spotted them coming down the road. Over a hundred head of cattle worked their way towards her at a steady trot. Some of the slower, older cows took a slow, steady pace at the end of the herd.

As they drew near, Sara became increasingly uneasy. She'd never been around anything so large that wasn't reign broke. Allowing the animals to go so freely made Sara feel uneasy — especially since the scene at the auction ring and rodeo were still so fresh in her mind.

She pressed herself close to the pickup, ready to leap in if one of the cattle so much as glanced at her in a threatening way. Thundering by, their hooves kicked up clouds of dust.

Finally, the last one passed leaving in their wake a roadway of half-moon footprints and a splattered of manure.

That evening, John treated Sara to a dinner on the prairie. Together, the two watched the sun droop towards the land like a flaming red yo-yo held by a heavenly hand.

The calm, balmy air made Sara relaxed. She found herself fighting to keep her eyes from drooping shut. John, too, appeared relaxed, tired from the weeks work. The two sat in silence, looking at the horizon.

"The sunset is so much more impressive here," Sara thought lazily. "It is as big and as beautiful as Nebraska.

After they backed up their meal and made their way to the car, both were rejuvenated.

"I've got an idea," John said. "Are you up for some dancing?"

"Well, I don't know," Sara said slowly. "Oh, I guess it sounds like fun. Let's go!"

Hopping into the car, the duo drove down a twisting road for several miles. Eventually, they came to a large wooden barn that was surrounded with vehicles.

"Get ready to have some fun — country style," John said, smiling.

They entered the large building and found it full of people. Dancers on the hardwood floor followed the bands lead, switching from a square dancing to a few country-western tunes. After several minutes of watching, John grabbed hold of Sara's hand.

"O.K. Let's go show 'em what we've got!," he said, pulling Sara towards the dance floor as she protested mildly.

All of Sara's years in Hidden Valley's exclusive social arena could not prepare her for country western dancing. Looking at those around her, Sara noted their motions were smooth and continuous. At first, she found herself pitifully off-tempo, unable to get the correct rhythm. After about three dances, she was beginning to get the hang of it, but was almost ready to call it quits.

As the music ended, John's friend Pete Janes came up and tapped John on the shoulder.

"John, what in the world are you doing to this lovely young lady? Trying to step on her feet? Maybe you could share her for a while and give this poor woman a break."

John laughed good-naturedly and asked Sara if she would mind. After a brief break, the music started once again and John stepped back as Pete began twirling Sara across the floor.

Despite her missteps, Pete remained good-natured, chatting lightly and telling jokes as they moved. After a few more times around the dance floor another of John's friends stepped in and again Sara was swept across the room.

When the band stopped for a break, Sara's dance partner helped her find John in the crowd. He was standing beside a gleaming redwood bar, exchanging laughter with a few friends.

John bought Sara a soda. The two broke away and found a seat near the dance floor.

"Why, I thought you'd abandoned me, John Olson."

"You seemed to be having a nice time. Besides, I'm not the best dance partner in the neighborhood."

"Well, you seem pretty good to me." The music began wafting through the air once again. This time, the music held the slow, sweet refrain of an old-time waltz. Taking John's hand, Sara stood and motioned towards the dance floor.

Sara noticed her feet behaved better during the slow songs. Around the dance floor they floated gracefully, the surrounding lights spinning like pinwheels. As they made small-talk, Sara was again impressed with John's easy-going nature. Their laughter flowed easily, as if their friendship stretched back years instead of just a few short months.

"Bet you've never met a girl that actually had two left feet, before."

"Oh, I think you've caught on fast enough. It's not easy to learn the dance of the cow-pokes. We've all had years to get it right."

"Now, you just wait. You'll get a real treat when you come out to New York for a visit. Then you'll be doing my style of dancing."

"What?!" John looked at his feet in mock surprise. "And kick off some of this good Nebraska dust?"

"Oh, now I know it would be a horrible shock. But you know the old saying—to those who much is given, much is expected in return." Nudging John gently, she leaned in closer to his ear. "And I will be expecting some return."

Moving back, she smiled slyly. John retaliated by twirling her around rapidly three times and then dropping her into a quick dip. Smiling victoriously, John pulled her back up into a standing position, Sara laughing breathlessly.

For the remainder of her time with them, the Olson's planned a trip to the Black Hills. Traveling light, the foursome piled into the Olson's trusty green car and set out to see one of the most sparsely-inhabited areas of Nebraska.

Sara was completely amazed at the vast nothingness of the land that surrounded her. In New York, it was rare to see an uninhabited area. Even in the parks, people milled around constantly. But here, there was nothing. Nothing but miles and miles of dirt and rocky land. Had it not been for the companionship of her fellow travelers, Sara would have felt a sense of dread from the extreme emptiness of the place.

They returned by way of the Badlands. While beautiful, Sara had a hard time envisioning anybody choosing to live in such a desolate area. She was glad to return to the Olson's as their seven-day adventure drew to a close.

John and Sara rounded out her last day in Nebraska with a trip to a canyon area. John hooked up a team of horses up to a wagon, and the duo set out down the bumpy country road.

Gradually, John steered the team down a gentle embankment. Alongside the widening trail, cattle grazed lazily and basked in the mid-morning sun. As they chatted back and forth, Sara didn't realize how far they had dropped in elevation until she glanced up to see their wagon dwarfed by massive walls of rock on either side.

"You know, a river once went through here," John said, pulling the horses to a stop. "It's hard to believe, isn't it—this area once completely under water."

Following John's lead, Sara got out of the wagon. Examining the rock closely, she noticed an occasional fossilized remain of some ancient sea creatures. Running her fingers along the small indentations, she studied them intently. The message they held was distant, spoken in a long-forgotten tongue. The tales of which they spoke were of a time and place so distant, her mind could not comprehend. Their presence may have been denied if not for this lasting reminder— impressions in stone, a lasting testament of their existence.

Sara walked down the empty creek bed, gently running her fingers along the rocks. For a long time she was silent, trying to visualize the river at its peak. She imagined it surrounded by layers of plush green vegetation. Enormous fish would have lumbered through the water, oblivious to the fact their lifeblood would one day be reduced to a trickle and, finally, sucked up entirely by a thirsty bed of dust.

The pair spoke sparingly, in hushed whispers. As Sara wandered ahead of the wagon to explore, John sat on a large boulder. He spotted a weary salamander nestling beneath a nearby rock. Grabbing a small pebble, he threw it, trying to get a response. But his aim was not true. Determined, John decided to make a game of it, flicking a handful of pebbles at the lazy amphibian one at a time.

John had been to this canyon often. At first, he was fascinated by it. But through the years, he had come to take advantage, viewing it as something commonplace. Like an old windmill or tree along the roadside, it had become ordinary but comforting. The awe and amazement it once drew from him had passed. As he quietly observed Sara's reaction, he found those old feelings of wonderment return. John was content to watch as Sara discovered something that was as much a part of his life as breathing.

John's thoughts wandered aimlessly, lulled by the canyons somber stillness. About to toss another pebble, he suddenly froze, his senses becoming alert. The horses, usually content, began beating their hooves against the rocky soil nervously. As their muscled backs quivered in readiness, the bridled pair whinnied in soft, muted tones, comforting each other against some unseen danger.

John walked quickly towards the wagon. Holding a bridled head securely, he checked on Sara's location. She had wandered about 40 feet ahead and was studying a rock formation with interest.

Scanning the canyon, nothing seemed unusual. A small group of cattle had wandered into a narrow clearing and were munching casually on a few sparsely scattered clumps of grass. Not wanting to panic, John fought back the urge to call Sara back—yet every instinct screamed out in warning. Deciding it wasn't worth the risk, John took a deep breath, ready to shout Sara's name.

As he did so, he caught a slight movement in rocks beyond Sara. At once, John froze, his voice dead in his throat. Between two large boulders, crouched the tense body of a prairie wolf. The thick, muscular hunter eyed a newborn calf possessively as it crouched to strike. Oblivious to his presence, Sara was unknowingly drifting closer to the wild animal.

As if she was reading his thoughts, Sara glanced at John briefly. His expression alarmed her. Following his frantic hand signals, she turned in the direction of the brown-coated hunter.

Discouraged by a lack of vegetation, the small group of cattle had began to move away. Frustrated his prey would escape, the prairie wolf crouched down menacingly, ready to utilize the element of surprise for his advantage. But the seasoned hunter remained cautious. Experience had been a good teacher, proving stealth and cunning earned the greatest prize.

Aware of the danger to Sara, John slowly walked to the wagon, drawing out a 22-caliber rifle. A trusted companion, John seldom ventured into the prairie without it. While the land provided him with a livelihood, it was still a wild place. John and those living there had frequent run-ins with the area's natural predators.

For the most part, they were harmless. But being unprepared could make the difference between life and death. Returning to his position in front of the horses, he motioned for Sara to move towards him. John looked through the gun's scope, setting the cross hairs on the wolf.

Sara slowly edged away from the canyon wall. A shiver crept up her spine, raising the hair on her neck. After making two steps she peered back over her shoulder. The prairie wolf seemed oblivious to anything but its escaping prey. With eyes trained on John, she quickened her pace.

Without warning, her foot caught a twisted root, throwing her to the ground. As she fell Sara screamed in surprise, falling hard on her hands and knees. Rolling onto her back, she involuntarily reached for her bruised ankle.

The surprised prairie wolf turned in alarm. Aware of being exposed it crouched down reflexively, ready to spring. Trapped between the canyon wall and Sara, its exits were blocked. With keen, golden-brown eyes the desperate hunter stared sullenly, gauging its next move. For a moment its fearless gaze locked with Sara, sending shockwaves of vulnerability throbbing through her veins.

John watched the wolf intently through the gun scope. There was no telling what the animal's next move might be. In order to get to Sara, it would have to leap over at least one large boulder. But trying to take the animal down where it was would be risky. A bullet could easily ricochet off the rocks and injure Sara. John knew timing would be everything. He watched as the prairie wolf's muscular ribcage gently rose and fell. A few drops of perspiration glistened on its slightly flared nostrils.

The three of them waited, trapped in a triangle of life and death. Sara forced her breath in and out, willing herself to remain calm. Ever so slowly, she found her feet, bringing them up slowly. As if commanding itself, her body slowly arose. Step by step, Sara backed towards John, each second lasting an eternity.

As Sara put more distance between herself and the wolf, John's finger tightened on the trigger. The animal was desperate now. John could feel it. Sara froze as a low, angry growl electrified the lifeless air.

In a breathless second the frantic animal made its move. Lurching forward in a single, fluid movement the wolf propelled itself atop a bolder. Hind legs pulsating with energy, it positioned itself to strike. As it sprang into the air a single shot rang out, echoing through the canyon walls. A flock of blackbirds nesting in a nearby tree flew upwards, wings flapping frantically. Midair, the prairie wolf's carcass fell limp, struck fatally in the breast. In slow motion, its viral body arched gracefully downward, landing on the ground with a thud.

Sara and John stared at the fallen beast speechlessly. Its fury extinguished, the prairie wolf's crumpled remains no longer commanded fear. But the close call left both John and Sara shaken.

John walked toward Sara. Gently, he put his arm around her waist and guided her towards the wagon. Overcome by waves of relief, Sara accepted his help and gingerly took a seat, trembling.

"Mr. Olson, that's just about all the excitement I care to have. I'm glad you're a good shot."

"I'm really sorry. I can't apologize enough. I've been down here many times and haven't even seen a ground squirrel."

"I guess I just bring you luck."

John rubbed his chin nervously. A clear picture of Sara's parents listening to stories about her trip to Nebraska formed in his mind.

"I'll bet most New Yorker's don't come back from vacation with a story like this."

Sara giggled a little too loudly.

"No. It's been pretty extraordinary. Not just this. The whole thing. But then, it seems like that's the way it usually is when we get together. We are magnets for adventure."

John had to admit, it was true. There was seldom a dull moment when Sara was around. When he thought of her returning to New York, and life returning to normal, his heart dropped.

"Well, I'd better be getting you back before something else comes crawling out of the rocks."

The ride back gave Sara time to calm down. When they returned back, it was time for Sara to finish packing. For the ride home, she chose a loose-fitting blouse and a pair of navy-blue pedal pushers.

Catching site of the high-heeled pumps she wore for her arrival, Sara chuckled quietly. "What must have John thought of me when I got off the train? I'm lucky he didn't send me right back home!"

Her train was scheduled to depart at 5:00 p.m. After a quick bite to eat, Sara gathered her things and brought them downstairs for John to load in the car. As she set them down, Ed and Helen came out of the kitchen to say their final farewells.

"Sara, you've been like a breath of fresh air these past couple weeks. If you ever feel like you need a break from the big city, feel free to come for a visit again. We'd love to have you," Helen said, giving Sara a hug.

When Helen moved away, Ed grabbed Sara's hand and began pumping it up and down enthusiastically.

"The next time we need someone to drive a tractor for bailing, we'll be sure and give you a call. Oh. I almost forgot. I made this up for you."

Ed handed Sara a neatly folded piece of paper. Examining it, Sara saw the names of several people. After a few seconds, she realized it was a family tree.

"I thought you might like to know a little more about the guy who wrote that diary you found. Kind of see where he fit in the grand scope of things. If it hadn't been for his adventuresome spirit, we would have never ended up here. He changed the lives of this family forever. I owe that man a great deal, and I thank you again for finding the piece of history that records it all," Ed said.

Sara graciously accepted Ed's gift. Carefully, she refolded the paper and slipped it into her purse. As John grabbed up Sara's bags, she gave each of her hosts one last hug and headed for the car.

The ride to the train station was silent, both John and Sara consumed with their own thoughts. As they parked near the train depot, Sara was roused from her reflections.

"Now, John Olson, don't you forget your promise. I will be expecting you to visit me—and soon. I don't think my itinerary will be nearly as exciting as yours was. But I just may have a few tricks up my sleeve."

"Oh, I'm sure you will, Miss Morris. I'm sure things will slow down sometime his summer. I'll give you a call when I can get away."

"Well. Then. I guess this is it. It's been a pleasure, John. I've really had a wonderful time."

Sara moved to get out of the car, and John followed suit, unlocking the trunk and carrying her bags to the depot. As Sara got her ticket, the train whistle sounded. She was just about to make a mad dash for the passenger car, when she stopped and turned toward John. In a quick motion, she hugged him hard and gave him a quick peck on the cheek.

"Remember our deal," she said, smiling as she turned quickly on her heel.

A few minutes later, the train lurched into motion. The train left the depot with each waving goodbye. As suddenly as Sara Morris arrived, she was gone. John's heart sunk as the train disappeared in the distance, the whine of it's whistle sighing in the empty silence.

Chapter 7

Getting back into a routine was difficult for Sara after returning home. The trip to Nebraska showed her a slow, easy-going pace that was hard to let go of. Although her visit was short, she had become used to seeing a blanket of green capped by an endless expanse of blue sky.

She now found the straight ribbons of sidewalk and endless paved roads cold and unappealing. They seemed monotonous, like a scratched record playing the same melody over and over again. Crowds of people weaving about busy main streets were distant and removed. Their calloused attitudes grated Sara's patience, their boldness stinging unexpectedly.

Sara busied herself by sending out applications and interviewing for teaching jobs in the area. She discovered life after graduation had both good points and bad. No longer tied down to a demanding schedule, Sara was amazed at the amount of extra time on her hands. But the lack of demands also created a kind of complacency. Hours and days would drift by quickly, with little being accomplished. Sara found herself struggling to remain focused.

Teaching jobs in the New York area were somewhat easy to find. But Sara quickly realized any position she accepted would have hidden drawbacks. The sheer number of students in each classroom was overwhelming in the public school system. Interviewing in different schools, the hallways surrounded with endless rows of lockers, seemed to merge and blend together. Each boxy classroom looked drab and generic.Sara wondered if, after a time, the students would begin blending together as well.

Sara also investigated opportunities in smaller, private schools. But in most cases, the administrations in the private sector possessed a haughty, self-absorbed attitude that Sara was all too familiar with. Like her peers, she knew the same tone would spread throughout the student body.

At one point in her search, Sara returned home confused and frustrated. Pushing the heavy wooden door closed, she caught sight of her father working in his study.

"Hi, dad. What are you up to?," Sara said, propping herself up against the door jam.

"Oh! Sara. Come in. Have a seat. Oh, you know how it is. Coming from another interview?"

"Yes. But things aren't going like I planned."

"How so?"

"Well, it's just that when I graduated, I had all this enthusiasm. I thought I'd just jump right in and get busy. You know. Start things off on a positive note. But every time I come out of an interview, all I can do is think of what's wrong with the place."

"Sara, that's the whole purpose of an interview. Sizing things up. It's better that you identify potential problems than get caught in a situation you won't like later on."

"I'm just wondering if I didn't make a mistake already. I just don't know if I'm even cut out for this teaching thing. Maybe I'd better start looking into some business prospects."

"That was the whole idea behind getting a dual degree. But don't be so quick to cash in your dreams. Just give it some time. You might stumble across the right place when you least expect it."

"I hope so, dad. I really hope so."

***

After Sara left, John found the ranch to be unusually quiet. He missed seeing the routine of his life through the fresh eyes of a new comer. Without her interest, his work seemed mundane. He realized there was no one to share his thoughts with at the end of the day.

Even visiting his familiar haunts, John continued to be reminded of Sara's presence. Talking to friends, her name was repeatedly brought up. Many had questions about the attractive New York girl who was showing an interest in Nebraska. And several pointed out that, if John were lucky and thinking straight, he might have a chance with the pretty Miss Morris.

Despite the fact he missed his visitor, John brushed off his friends remarks. A realist, he thought it would be unlikely their relationship would develop beyond friendship. Their social differences, John reasoned, were glaring. There was no doubt Sara was accustomed to a much different lifestyle—one influenced heavily by money and affluence.

His desires and needs, on the other hand, were simple and common. His goal was to feel the full-bellied satisfaction of accomplishing a job with his own hands, and being proud enough of his accomplishments to stand behind his work.

Yes, Sara was a good friend. But she came from a world where people like John didn't have a place.

Still, he had to admit that she added a dimension to his life that was lacking. The culture, the excitement—everything good about New York and financial affluence was embodied in Sara. She was a good friend, and for that John was grateful. But he knew that sometimes, that was the most two people could become. And, John thought with conviction, that would be enough for him.

Embracing that friendship when possible was important to John. As he worked, he quietly planned to make good on his promise to visit Sara in New York. Despite his negative war-time experiences in the Big Apple, John found himself looking forward to it. This time, he would get to experience the city with someone he enjoyed. The war now just a distant memory, much of the anxiety would also be gone. He might even enjoy it. For the first time he would be able to see the city as others did—share their wonderment of its varied sites and sounds. And with Sara running the show, John knew he would see the city at its best.

As the spring work load lessened, thoughts about Sara and New York returned to John often. During a late-June lull he decided to give Sara a call.

A formal, masculine voice answered the phone. A few minutes later, the familiar melody of Sara's voice rang out.

"Hello," Sara answered breathlessly.

"Hello, stranger. What were you doing?"

"John! Nice to hear you're voice. Oh, not much, really. I actually just walked in. One of mother's clubs is helping organize some July 4 festivities. I got roped into helping."

"Planning on having a big celebration?"

"Oh, you know. The usual. There will be a big fireworks display. And a barbecue. Probably a lot of mosquitoes, too. So, what do you have on your mind?"

John paused, knowing Sara was expecting a significant announcement.

"Thoughts of New York. Maybe visiting a young lady friend I know there."

"Really?," Sara said, then lowered her voice "She must be quite a lucky girl."

John laughed loudly.

"So when might this visit be forthcoming?"

"I guess it depends on how busy my lady friend is."

"Oh, stop it, John. The suspense is killing me. When are you coming down?"

"Well, I was going to see about next week. But I realize it's short notice ..."

"Are you kidding? That would be perfect! You haven't seen New York until you've seen our fine Independence Day celebrations."

"Well, good. It's settled then. I'll try making arrangements to leave here in a couple days. That means I will probably arrive there on ... July 3rd. Will that work out?"

"Yes! Let me know what time and I'll meet you at Grand Central."

After saying quick good-byes, John dropped the phone back onto the cradle. A pleased smile inched its way across his face.

Days later, John boarded the now-familiar train headed east. As he made the two-and-a-half day trip, he had plenty of time to think. He'd been on this journey before, but always ended up at the waterfront or harbor. There had always been a ship there, waiting impatiently to take him away from the country he called home. The anxiety of those days came flooding back. Not knowing how each mission would conclude was a constant burden.

Would this experience be better? Again, he would be facing the unknown. This time a world of affluence awaited. Once again, he would need to struggle to fit in. Like a bull running loose in a China shop, he could do irreparable damage to his friendship with Sara if not careful.

John's fears continued to grow as he drew closer to New York. His only solace was in his parents parting words, "We are what we are and so be it."

When he did finally arrive at Grand Central Station, John was again surprised by the large crowds milling around. For a moment he panicked, worried he would not find Sara in the crush. A rush of relief swept over him as he spotted her next to the wall. She stood on a wooden milk crate dressed in a bright red dress. In her hand she waved a sizable piece of blue material. As John drew closer, he realized the cloth was really a Nebraska state flag.

Sara greeted John with a generous hug. After they broke apart, he examined the flag more closely.

"Where in the world did you come up with this?," John shouted over the crowd's din.

"What do you mean? This is New York! Here, anything is possible," Sara said, turning to exit the crowded station.

Sara showed John to a shiny, new car parked close by. They slid into the wide, spacious back seat.

"I thought I'd better have Merle drive us. There's no way I would have found a parking space down here," she said.

After a few quick introductions, their car pulled away from the curb and entered the stubborn flow surrounding them.

"So, how was your trip?," Sara said, moving a sweaty lock of hair behind her ear.

"Oh, I guess it wasn't so much different than a month ago. Far. Slow. Boring." John felt his old feelings of insecurity creeping back.

"Yes, it's a long trip, all right. But you know what? I'm glad you're here. Things were boring without you."

John temporarily forgot the uncomfortable way his polyester shirt clung against his sticky body.

"That's nice of you to say. But I don't think New York is the kind of place a person can stay bored for very long."

"Yes, there are things to do here. Of course, it can't compare to the excitement of looking a prairie wolf in the eyes—although things here can get a little wild now and then. You know, there aren't a lot of nice people to hang around with. You know—normal people."

"Do you think I'm normal? Well, a lot you know!"

John felt himself relaxing. The tight, uncomfortable polyester shirt seemed to loosen and become more roomy. He turned towards Sara.

"So, what have you got planned for me?"

"Well, actually, my parents and I have given this a lot of thought. We got together and drew up a list of ideas. You can look them over and see what you're interested in. And I, of course, will be your faithful host regardless of what you choose."

An hour later, Sara and John arrived at the Morris home. When they entered, Joe and Agnes were seated in the study, awaiting dinner. After a few brief introductions, Mrs. Morris called for Merle who was just bringing John's suitcase in through the servants entrance.

"Merle, won't you be a dear and show Mr. Olson to his room. I'm sure he would like to freshen up before we dine," Agnes said. As John ascended the staircase, she studied him with narrowed eyes.

Merle opened the door of John's room in a single, smooth motion. If he needed anything, John was instructed to push a button on the wall which would sound in the servants kitchen. Bowing down graciously, Merle left the room.

For a few minutes, John simply stood, awed by the luxury surrounding him. A burgundy bedspread with a thick brocade pattern exactly matched the cushioned seat of a plush armchair placed near the window. Velvet curtains, the same color as the bedspread, were pulled back to reveal a colorful garden below. Against the wall stood a dressing table guarded by a huge gilded mirror.

Walking to the adjacent bathroom, John was surprised by the carpet's marshmallow-like feel. He found it difficult to walk on its luxurious, inviting surface. Standing in the bathroom's doorway, John was again astounded. The bedroom carpet ended, giving way to gleaming beige marble. A double-basined lavatory of the same marble was punctuated by sparkling gold faucets. Another large mirror, this one almost taking up the entire wall, was positioned above. Ornate lights with painstakingly-cut crystal created gentle prisms.

Sitting in the center of the room was an immense claw-footed bathtub. A beige curtain in delicate lace encircled the massive porcelain centerpiece for use with the attached shower.

After washing his hands and face, John dried his face with a thirsty monogrammed towel. Carefully, he tucked it back into place on the towel rack, smoothing it out carefully before leaving.

A few minutes later, John came downstairs freshly dressed. Joe handed him a glass of sherry, and the group seated themselves for dinner.

The very properly-served, four-course dinner went along well, in fact, far beyond John's expectations. In a short time, the Morris family put him at ease, talking about Independence-day festivities that would be taking place the next day. They asked John about what activities took place in North Platte. From there, the conversation moved to a discussion about Nebraska.

Afterwards, Mr. and Mrs. Morris retired for the evening and Sara and John were left to their own devices. They gravitated to a gazebo in the back yard.

"So, what do you think?," Sara said, hedging.

"Very nice. You've got a very nice place here."

"Thanks. But I was really asking about my parents."

"They seem nice, too."

Sara threw her head back, laughing. "Oh come on. It's me you're talking to. You don't have to be so nice."

John leaned forward, resting his elbows on his knees. "I'm not being nice. That's what I think. They're nice."

Sara crossed her arms as she stared at some nearby flowers. The midsummer sun had sunk low in the sky making long shadows in the garden.

"I guess you're right. I mean, you really haven't had a chance to get to know mother yet. She can get kind of pushy."

John smiled. "I think that's a good mother's job. She only wants the best for you, I'm sure."

"How does she know what's best for me?"

"I don't know. Experience, maybe?"

Sara scowled slightly, ready to change the topic. "So, what would you like to do during your big New York vacation?"

"I'm open to suggestions. When we were docked during the war, I really wasn't up for a lot of sight-seeing. I'm sure I'll find anything interesting."

"Well, then I guess we'd better turn in. We'll start bright and early tomorrow morning."

***

As promised, Sara was up and ready to go early the next morning. After a large, delicious breakfast served in the Morris' sunny breakfast nook, Sara and John headed for the garage.

"There are going to be some sail-boat races on the waterfront today. It's being held in conjunction with a big multicultural fair. It should be fun," Sara said.

Because they set out early, traffic in the city was still manageable. Seeming to know where she was going, Sara snaked around streets surrounded by massive skyscrapers. Following Roosevelt Drive South, she followed the Manhattan coastline.

Nearing East River Drive along Manhattan's southern edge, congestion became a significant problem. Sara entered a garage labeled "private." After a few brief words with the guard on duty at the gate, she drove in and quickly found a spot.

"Dad's company has these lots reserved. We'll have to walk, but at least the car will be here when we're done."

Together, Sara and John made their way through the crowded streets. John had forgotten how busy this place was—forgotten what it was like to be alone in a sea of people.

Eventually, the smell of sweet, spicy food met John's nostrils. Curbside venders lined the streets with rows of colorful knickknacks and goods. A wide woman dressed in an orange and yellow kimono and boxy brown hat sat in a booth surrounded with seashell necklaces and bracelets. Next to her was a stand of fragile, ornamental glassware overseen by a tiny, black-haired oriental woman who spoke in a foreign tongue. Next, white-faced mimes were engaged in a playful pantomime, an obtrusive donation box bolted securely to a heavy wooden chair.

So it went, down both sides of the street for several blocks. Sara and John took their time, venturing into the makeshift stalls that interested them. At one point, Sara found a pretty pair of pearl earrings that caught her fancy, which John promptly bought. For fun, John tried on a brightly-colored Mexican poncho. After some quick bartering in Spanish, Sara handed John the garment.

Leaving the stand, John glanced at his host, surprised. The only people John had heard speak in foreign tongues were older North Platte residents who clung to their European roots. Germans, Czechs and Poles who used their language like a kind of secrete code, mostly to talk around their children when the subject under discussion was inappropriate for young ears. John knew Sara's ability was not casually passed on, but learned from careful study.

Bending down to her ear, John shouted over the commotion.

"I'm impressed."

"Don't be. Mrs. Cortez' Spanish class was mandatory."

After a few hours of milling around, Sara grabbed John's hand and pulled him into a small cafe. A couple was just leaving, and Sara headed straight for their empty seats.

A few seconds later, an olive-skinned woman woman dressed in a tight red and black dress brought them menus. John recognized many of the dishes as favorites of his former Italian ship-mates. He settled on a mild tomato pasta, wary of the other dishes. Following John's lead, Sara also stuck to a lighter fare.

After eating they headed for the dock. A number of boats were coasting in the distance. Brightly- colored sails strained to catch a gentle breeze. Sara and John each picked their favorite. John chose to root for a sleek, white boat with a sky-blue sale. The name "Ocean Boy" was painted on the boats hull in bold letters. Sara, on the other hand, liked a slightly larger boat. Its bright, dandelion-yellow sail stood out from the others. The name "Gabriel" graced the boat in a fine, arching script.

About 30 boats skimmed atop the water, finding their place along the starting line. With the sudden crack of a gun, they began skimming across the water.

Surrounding John and Sara, fans cheered on their favorite entry. Grabbing John's hand, Sara led him out of the crowd. Together they ran toward a bridge overlooking the bay. They pushed their way between the crowd, arriving just in time to watch the boats glide effortlessly below them.

As they traveled into the distance, the cowboy and the lady kept their favorites in sight. They took turns ribbing each other when Gabriel or Ocean Boy inched ahead.

For several minutes, the boats almost disappeared from sight, just so many dots on the horizon. But eventually their shapes became recognizable again. Sara leapt in joy when her favorite boat pulled ahead of the pack. But in a short while, Ocean Boy came from the rear, overtaking those in the lead.

Nearing the finish line, Sara and John's boats were neck and neck. Both watched anxiously for the outcome. Fifty feet before the finish line, John's favorite finally took the lead. But Gabriel reacted by picking up its pace slightly. When the race ended, it took a few moments for official news of the winner to make its way through the crowd. Their questions were answered when a bright white flare blossomed above the Gabriel.

Sara cheered happily, jumping with joy and giving John a hug. Caught up in the excitement, John laughed, giving Sara credit for picking the winner from afar.

The crowd on the bridge began to leave, but John and Sara lingered on. The location gave them a wonderful view of the shoreline. The crowded street vendors blended into a mosaic of color. Most of the boats were returning to the dock, but others continued to sail. Light and carefree, they looked like butterflies flirting on a bed of blue.

Slowly, regretfully, Sara and John began to break away. Walking back toward the sidewalk vendors, John thought plaintively about how he would think of this day often after he returned home. It would stand out as he flipped through the scrapbook of images in his mind. What made this day so special to him was unclear. But he was grateful to have Sara by his side to share it.

The duo ambled by the anxious venders, the excitement of their wares now lacking urgency. Like a babbling brook's soothing flow, the sound of their voices traveled over them, lulling them into contentment. It was enough for them to be in the center of the frenzied activity, the frantic energy that was New York. Becoming a part of it wasn't necessary — their job was simply to be there and enjoy it.

Darkness slowly crept over the city. John bought hot dogs and drinks from a portly, rosy-cheeked vender. He and Sara found a bench and ate their dinner, looking out on New York City Harbor. People milled around, some carrying lawn chairs and others staking out grassy spots with blankets. As John and Sara were about to call it a day, the sky exploded with an electric cascade of fireworks.

Sara ooed and ahhhd at the gaudy display. John was surprised at the celebrations intensity and sat back to enjoy it fully. The fireworks steady blossom illuminated ships in the harbor. As the sky lit repeatedly, John's thoughts slowed, the steady shower of lights washing over him like a soothing balm.

The display ended with a massive cannon report and for a moment the whole city seemed to hold its breath. With a sudden burst of exuberance the harbor boats exploded with a symphony of horns. High pitched wines sang along with the low bass grumble of sturdy tugs.

All around them, the city suddenly seemed to come alive. A steady stream of cars inched by on nearby West Street, some honking horns in tune with the harbor symphony. Calling out, they announced their departure from the festivities. And while many would continue to celebrate well into the night, Sara and John realized it was time for them to call it a day.

Wearily they walked toward the parking lot that held Sara's car. On the way they passed the area where venders had lit up the street earlier. Now, it was dark and abandoned. Curbside lights shone down like spotlights on a vacant stage. A few empty cardboard boxes and random papers were the only evidence of the play's final scene.

Long shadows followed John and Sara as they walked, causing them to quicken their steps. At last they reached the parking garage. Now, a different guard was on duty. As they drew closer, the newspaper in his hands rustled as he peered suspiciously over the top. A plume of pungent-spelling smoke slithered from a cigar hanging limply from his stubbled face. After a brief, disapproving look he went back to his paper distractedly.

The lot was still full of cars, but otherwise abandoned. John was glad to see Sara's car waiting where they left it. They slid into its soft, spacious interior and sat for a moment, relieved by the sense of security it offered. Eventually, Sara started the engine and backed it out of the stall. The traffic had become considerably lighter, but the trip out of town was still slow.

John studied the skyscrapers flanking the roadway on either side. So many people, the only way to go was up. Being away from it had made John forget slightly. He looked on it with a mixture of awe and cynicism—much like the New Yorkers he met during the war.

Gradually, the number of cars they shared the road with dropped to a trickle. Traveling on the expressway, John couldn't see much of the houses beyond. Most looked like cookie-cutter replicas. At one point, faint streetlights reflected rough, ramshackle, houses with peeling paint and tin roofs.

Sara turned off the main road, and the homes began to be spaced further apart. Their grandeur improved, spacious front lawns and dramatic entryways gradually becoming commonplace. John was surprised when they slowed and pulled into Morris' driveway. The place looked different in the dark, the days fatigue clouding his judgment.

When they opened the front door, Sara threw her keys down on a telephone table in the foyer and turned her attention to John.

"You didn't say much on the way home."

"It was a busy day. A nice day—but a busy day. It brought back a lot of memories."

"About the war, you mean."

John's mind flashed back to his earliest impressions of New York—its impersonal vastness. Mixed in was something else, as well. Although he hadn't acknowledged it before, John now knew how to label that ambiguous, ominous presence that had dominated his connection to New York.

It was fear, pure and simple. Fear of leaving home for the unknown, fear of striking out on his own in a new place, fear of a watery death at sea.

For years, John's apprehension was connected to New York like an unseverable umbilical cord. Even after returning to Nebraska, the old feeling followed him like a shadowy ghost with no name.

Returning had made those feelings resurface. It was exhausting to face his emotions once again. Yet somehow, Sara had driven those old feeling back, drowning them in the watery depths he once feared.

Looking at Sara, he realized she would never completely understand his ambivalence toward her native city. Yet somehow, her presence made it all irrelevant. The distance Sara put between John and his past made it easier to examine and deal with his feelings. Although he didn't realize it until now, he was ready to do just that.

"Yes. The war. But I can honestly say New York never looked better than it did with you by my side today. It will always be a fond memory."

"Well, good. I guess that's not bad for a first day. Tell you what. I'm exhausted, so I'm going to head to bed. Let's not worry about getting an early start tomorrow morning—we could both use the rest. We'll do something a little closer to home tomorrow and just take it easy."

"Sounds good. See you in the morning."

Sara and John went to their rooms. As John laid on his bed staring up at the ceiling, he allowed the wartime images to run through his mind like a grainy black and white picture show. As each painful memory played out, John bid it farewell, exiling the heartache it created.

As the sun breathed life into the eastern sky John slept peacefully, his demons banished to the past. He was now released and free to enjoy the gift that was his life.

When he awoke, John's eyes focused on the nightstand clock wearily. It was 10:30 a. m. Shocked, he leapt out of bed and took a quick shower. When he entered the breakfast room, he was relieved to see that Sara was just sitting down to read the morning newspaper.

"Good morning, sleepy head," Sara said, putting the paper down and taking a drink of orange juice.

"Good morning yourself. Looks like we both got a late start today."

"Yes, I guess the Nebraska boy did a good job of tiring out the New York girl. So, you see, I've got an excuse."

"That's where I come up short—no excuses for me. But things look much brighter today. The extra rest did me good. So, what does my tour guide have in store for me today."

"A little Nebraska-style fun. Thought we'd drive up to the stables. Figured you might like to see some of our animals, being used to riding horses and all."

John agreed enthusiastically. After a light breakfast Sara went into the kitchen to get a picnic basket. Their car was waiting in front of the house, gas tank refilled. Instead of going east, Sara turned west and drove for about half an hour. Turning onto a rural road, John was surprised to discover such an open area existed so near New York City. Neatly groomed houses were placed at spacious intervals, some surrounded by white fences, others centered neatly on emerald green lawns.

After driving a few more miles Sara turned into a narrow lane. A sign post bearing the name "Willow Acres" bridged the well-manicured roadway.

They traveled about a quarter of a mile before the stable came into view. A long white building flanked by a large riding ring dominated the yard. Across from it was a small, well kept house, undoubtedly where the horses groomers lived.

After parking the car, Sara strolled to the stable door and opened it as if she'd done it many times before. She motioned for John to follow as she made her way to a chestnut-colored mare.

"This is my favorite. Dad gave her to me about five years ago as a birthday present." Sara stroked the horses soft nose gently. "Isn't she great?"

John, distracted by the stables generous size and bright, clean stalls didn't answer. Across from the mare a black stallion pranced about nervously. John drew near and looked into the animals large black eyes, keeping his hands in his pockets.

"What's the story with this one?," he asked.

"Well, this is actually one dad just bought. His name is Thunderbolt. He has an excellent blood line and dad is hoping to use him as a stud. The problem is, he's so high strung we haven't really gotten comfortable with him yet."

"Yes, he looks pretty high strung. Is he a runner?"

"A quarter horse. He could have been a racer, but just didn't have the disposition. Too hard headed. Would you like to take him out and have a look?"

After a moments careful thought, John agreed. Sara grabbed a rope and hooked it onto Thunderbolt's halter. Holding him firmly, she led him into the adjacent outdoor riding arena.

John studied the stallion carefully as it shimmied restlessly from side to side. It eyed its human companions suspiciously.

"I think whoever broke him was heavy-handed. Some horses just won't tolerate that. Gives 'em a bad impression of humans that just never goes away."

John walked beside Thunderbolt, stroking him gently. As he did so, the horse turned his head curiously. The animals dark coat took on a blue hue in the sunlight. Speaking softly, John made his way to the horses legs and examined them carefully. Tugging gently, John prompted the animal to left its hooves, which it did reluctantly. Finally, taking a deep breath, John stepped away.

"This is quite a horse. Mind if I take it for a ride?"

"Are you sure?"

"Sure. We Nebraska boys like to live dangerously."

With a slight shake of her head Sara headed into the stable for the riding gear. A few minutes after she returned, the horse was ready to go.

"O.K., here goes nothing," John said, slipping his foot into a stirrup.

Initially, Thunderbolt resisted, protesting softly as its front hooves danced into the air. But John hung on stubbornly as he continued to speak in soft, muted tones. Suddenly, the horse began running at full speed, throwing up clouds of dust behind him. He completed two frantic circles before finally slowing down.

Reigning sharply, John headed Thunderbolt towards Sara, who had been watching in interest.

"Well, are you ready for a ride?," John said.

"Not on that one, thank you. I'll get Princess saddled up. If you're feeling brave, we can go check out some of the trails."

"Sounds good to me," John said.

A few minutes later Sara had her horse saddled and ready to go. After opening the corral gate, Sara and John headed for an open pasture area.

They spent the rest of the morning exploring the Morris acreage, the size of which surprised John. A wooded area with a small stream crossed over one section of the parcel, which John and Sara explored at length.

At noon, Sara tied her horse and started taking out the lunch she had transferred from the picnic basket. After they finished, John and Sara rested against some nearby trees, skipping rocks in the stream.

Soon after they headed back for the stable. Taking a direct path, Sara and John began to race as they neared their journey's end.

When they arrived back, the stable hand was in the process of feeding the other horses.

"Hi, Frankie," Sara said, breathless from the ride. "Looks like we found somebody to handle Thunderbolt. He never gave John a bit of trouble."

The wiry, salt-and-pepper haired stable man smiled agreeable, reaching for Sara's reigns as she dismounted.

"Looks like old Thunderbolt just likes to feel his oats. Likes to have nothing but open space ahead of him," John said, dismounting and stroking the animals neck.

"Frankie, could you be a dear and take care of these horses. I told dad I'd try to be back before 3:00."

"Sure, no problem," Frankie said agreeably, leading the animals back into the stable.

"Do you and your dad have something special planned?," John asked.

"Well, actually, yes, although nothing was set in stone. Dad offered to take you golfing. I mean, if we got back in time."

"Golfing! Now, that's something I've never done before. Are you sure your dad won't be embarrassed to bring somebody like me around?"

"Oh, heavens no. Dad likes the game, but it's all in fun. I think he just wants to talk to you anyway. You know, man to man stuff."

John didn't know what to think of Sara's remark, although it did make him curious. But Sara had always spoken highly of her father, so John could see no problem with it.

They arrived back at the house just in time. Joe was walking out the door as they drove up.

"Well, John, I'd love to have you come along, if you'd like. But there's no pressure if you've got something else in mind," Joe said.

John immediately went upstairs to change into fresh clothes. Less than fifteen minutes later, Joe and John were pulling into the Rolling Acres Country Club. Joe quickly arranged for two caddies and in a short time the pair was teeing off.

Joe gave John some basic pointers, then handed John a golf ball. As John looked down at the small white object and eyed the distant hole, his thoughts chanted loudly in the background.

"Oh, great. What an impression I'm going to make. I've never even seen a golf club before, and I'm supposed to use it on this little ball. I should have my head examined," John fretted to himself.

John carefully drew his club back as Joe instructed and brought it down with a wallop. He was amazed to see the ball go sailing through the air in the approximate direction he had aimed. It bounced down about 25-feet from the hole.

"Not bad! Not bad at all!," Joe said enthusiastically. "The first time I played, the ball went in the opposite direction. Looks like you've got quite an arm."

The two exchanged small talk through the first five holes, each looking for some common ground.

"So you're a rancher," Joe ventured cautiously. "According to Sara, its quite a demanding job."

"Oh, yes. Well, it can be. Especially if the weather gets bad. And Sara saw it at about the worst."

"Is it worth it? I know you don't exactly get paid by the hour."

John considered the question carefully as Joe prepare to swing.

"It can if you know what your doing. A lot goes into raising cattle. If you know what to avoid, and when to do certain things, the animals thrive. With luck, you make a profit. But mistakes cost."

"You probably learned a lot from your father."

"Yes, parts of the ranch have been in our family for generations. I guess it's got to the point where ranching is in our blood."

"That's interesting," Joe said, stopping to consider John's words. "I don't think any of my ancestors were ever anything besides businessmen. Who knows. If they'd gotten a taste of it, we might be your neighbors in Nebraska right now."

Joe chuckled, pleased with his new understanding of John's background. But John, on the other hand, had a hard time envisioning Joe Morris doing anything but casually holding a golf club.

"So tell me," Joe continued, "Are you enjoying your trip to New York?"

"Yes, it looks like Sara's got everything all planned out. I've been enjoying her tour."

"Yes, my Sara knows her way around New York. Too bad she's so disillusioned with it."

"Disillusioned? In what way?"

"Oh, I probably shouldn't say anything, but she's admitted to me that she hasn't been having much luck job hunting. I think she's just become a fickle New Yorker. She just needs a little time to find her niche. It will come."

John had a hard time believing Sara would be having a hard time deciding on a job. But considering his own experiences in New York, he was not entirely surprised. He could understand her indecision and difficulty in making a decision.

When John and Joe returned home, Sara was waiting.

"So how did it go?," she asked.

"This guy has a wonderful swing. A little practice, and he'd be in with the pro's. Oh, before I forget. I was wondering if John might not like making a trip to the exchange sometime during his stay. He might be interested in seeing how the markets for his cattle are settled each day. It's really something everyone should do at least once."

"Thanks, daddy," Sara said, grabbing John's arm and directing him to the music room. "I'll take it under advisement."

With a laugh, Joe turned to walk up the steps. Sara motioned for John to have a seat on the plush, upholstered couch.

"So, how did it really go?"

"Great, your dad's a nice guy."

"No probing questions?"

"No, not really."

"Well, be grateful. Just wait until my mother gets a hold of you. Now, what would you like to do next?"

"I have no idea. But I am getting a little hungry."

"Wonderful. Tell you what. Why don't you get dressed and I'll take you out to eat. My treat."

"Oh, that's very New York of you. But really, I think I should take care of the bill. You pick the place."

"Done. Dress in your most grand attire, kind sir. And prepare for an evening of dinner and dancing," Sara said, waving her arms in mock grandeur.

Sara met John by the front door, coat already on. Her hair had been coiffed into an elegant French twist. Diamond teardrop earrings dangled from her lobes. John, on the other hand, sported his Sunday suit. One of the two he owned.

Sara had again enlisted Merle to act as chauffeur. He opened the door for Sara and John and then proceeded to drive to an exclusive club overlooking the Hudson River. As they stepped from their car, spirited music flowed out to greet them.

The club was lit with cascading chandeliers and white-linen tables accented by candlelight. In the center of the room was a large dance floor on which several couples swayed in graceful unison.

John noted most of the women wore pale dresses of sheer chiffon that flirted at knee length as they wafted through the room. The men, on the

116

other hand, sported black ties or suits that were much more up-to-date than the one John wore.

Turning to Sara to help her off with her coat, he was surprised to see her evening dress for the first time. Unlike the others, she wore a black strapless number that hugged her torso tightly. Her black layered chiffon skirt was sprinkled with small, glittering rhinestones that picked up the candles warm glow. Sara's delicate crystal earrings gave her face and eyes a soft, spirited blush.

The two were escorted to a table and given menus. Both hungry, they ordered quickly. When the waiter left, Sara leaned toward John mischievously.

"Don't you think it's a shame to waste a perfectly good dance just sitting here?"

John immediately picked up her cue, but was a bit apprehensive. This wasn't the kind of dancing he was accustomed to, and he wasn't thrilled about the prospect of embarrassing Sara in front of her friends.

Sara studied John's face carefully.

"Oh, I see. Well, you wait right here."

Sara pushed her chair back and found the maitre d'. The two spoke with heads bent close together for a few minutes, sharing some secret confidence. Then Sara returned and took her seat.

A few minutes later the song ended. The band began ruffling through their music and soon brought their instruments to their lips. The strains of a country-western waltz floated through the air.

John stood up offering Sara his hand and the two began moving smoothly around the dance floor. A little thrown off by the change, many dancers decided to take a seat, leaving the floor open for Sara and John. But John continued on, oblivious to the fact he and his partner had become the center of attention. He guided Sara across the dance floor, quite certain he had never seen anyone look so lovely. Her earrings glittered and reflected in her eyes.

Not until the music ended was the spell broken. John was surprised to see the floor had been abandoned and all eyes had been following them across the dance floor.

Sara, too, was caught off guard. But without a second of hesitation, decided to use the situation to her advantage. She quickly bowed into a deep curtsy, first in one direction and then another. Following her lead, John smiled widely. Bringing his right arm across his waist, he bowed down deeply. Amused, the onlookers began clapping lightly at first.

Soon, more people joined in and a few voices chanted "More! More!." Laughing, Sara shook her head and began heading back to their dining table.

As she and John were about to be seated, Sara caught some movement out of the corner of her eye. Glancing over a few tables, she was surprised to see her parents sitting at a table with another couple. Sara and John walked over.

"Mother! Dad! I had no idea you were planning to come here tonight."

"Yes, well that is quite obvious, dear," Agnes said.

"Actually," Joe cut in, "it was a last-minute decision. George and Adeline stopped by and we decided to go out."

"We were just in time to see your solo debut," Agnes quipped.

"Oh, how nice," Sara said, pretending not to have heard. "John, I would like to introduce you to George and Adeline Divine. Mr. and Mrs. Divine, this is my friend John Olson. He is visiting from Nebraska."

"Nice to meet you, son," George said. "Looks like you've got your dance steps down."

"Well, thank you, sir, but not really. I just had a very talented partner."

Sara caught site of the waiter bringing their food to the table.

"Well, I'm sorry to cut this short, but I see our dinners are being served. Please excuse us. Nice seeing you, daddy," Sara said, giving her father a quick peck on the cheek. Straightening, she looked at her mother steadily "Mother, do have a nice evening. George, Adeline, it's always a pleasure. Now, if you don't mind ..."

With a quick wave, Sara turned heel and headed back to their table, John following close behind. It had been hours since he'd eaten last, and John's stomach ground fitfully as he took his first forkful of food. After a few more bites, he paused.

"Mmmm. This is very good."

"That's because you worked for your dinner. Sorry about mother's remarks. She's a little — self conscious — around her friends."

"Oh, that's just because she doesn't want her beautiful daughter taking up with some old cow poke. Can't say as I blame her."

"Beautiful, huh?," Sara said, swirling her drink around with a straw. "Am I to think your hunger's made you lose your head? And what's this about you being a cow poke. I happen to think cow pokes are quite handsome."

"Ma'am," the waiter interrupted, "Is everything served to your satisfaction?"

"Oh, yes, very good. My compliments to the chef."

"And you, sir?"

"Yes. Thank you."

"Very good," the waiter said, bowing slightly as he left.

For a few minutes Sara and John ate in silence, each lost in their own thoughts. Just as Sara was about to speak, a tall, black haired young man rested his hand on her shoulder roughly.

"Well Sssara. Sssara Morris. My God. It's been a long time," he said, leaning in close.

Sara involuntarily moved away, the smell of his breath heavy with alcohol. Straining to get a good look at his face, she realized it was Chet Armstrong, a long-time family acquaintance.

It had been several years since she'd seen him last. Although she couldn't recall the exact details, Sara remembered he'd been involved in some corporate unpleasantness. While the facts were sketchy, she remembered it had something to do with misappropriating funds. He could have lost his job or even been jailed if his affluent father, a long-time politician and businessman, had not intervened.

Judging from his actions, Sara guessed his lack of character still prevailed.

"Why, don't tell me you've forgotten you're old buddy?," Chet said, staggering slightly.

"Of course not, Chet. So tell me, who are you here with this evening."

"Well, I know who I'm not with — the most lovely lady in the building. That honor would go to that man," Chet said, pointing to John.

"Well, John, I would like you to meet Chet Armstrong. Chet, this is my friend John Olson. He's visiting from Nebraska."

"Neebrasska. Neebrasska. Hmmm. Never heard of it. Oh, yea! I remember, now! Isn't that where they're always having all those Indian problems. You know — the Indians," Chet put his hand over his mouth, moving it back and fourth quickly several times as he let out a loud, high-pitched whoop.

John bristled slightly, but said nothing.

"Chet, for heavens sake. I had no idea you were a history buff," Sara said, raising her brows cynically.

"Oh, come on, Sara. Your friend can take a little ribbing. Oh! But this is starting to look like a little more than friendship. I saw you two on the dance floor—Sara and her Nebraska stud doing a cow-poke dance. That is what they call, it, isn't it ... Johnny."

Sara and John exchanged an uncomfortable glance.

"Maybe it would be a good time for you to get lost, Chet. I really don't have anything more to say to you," Sara said.

"Oh, come on. Don't be that way. Let me make it up to you with a dance. Just one."

Sara grimaced. "Really, Chet, I don't think so. I'm in the middle of my meal and, quite frankly, your so drunk you can barely walk, much less dance. I'd appreciate it if you'd just go back to wherever you came from."

Chet stood up sharply, his face hard. "I'm sure you can't be serious. You'd rather sit here with this, this—cowboy instead of dance with me? What, do you feel sorry for him? Is he your most recent charity case?"

Bending down close, he hissed menacingly, his breath scalding Sara's ear. "Come on, ditch him. I can take you places you've never gone before." Grabbing her arm, Chet tried to lift Sara from her seat.

"O.K., baby face, I think the lady's had enough. Just let go of her and leave us alone," John said, getting to his feet.

"Oooh. Cowboy knows how to talk tough. Well sorry, cowboy, I'm not buying. Do you have any idea of who you're talking to? I don't take orders, I give them. So why don't you just get your scrawny butt back to Indian country and quit trying to squirm in where you don't belong."

John's face began to flush.

"I told you to go back to your table," he said, moving closer to Chet, "and I suggest you do it."

"Forget it, cowboy," Chet said, shoving John backwards.

What happened next occurred so quickly, Sara had no time to react. Drawing back his arm, John delivered a quick right hook that squarely caught Chet's jaw. Although it temporarily disoriented him, Chet raised his arms defensively, preparing to land a return punch. Just as he let his right fist fly, John decked him under the chin with a firm upper cut.

For a moment, Chet stood there, dumbfounded. Then, his eyes suddenly rolled backwards and his entire body followed suite. He fell limply to the ground.

A stunned silence seemed to spread throughout the ballroom. Even the band, which had been playing a gay tune, stopped abruptly. A group of onlookers began rushing forward to revive the fallen reveler. A few diners seated nearby smirked quietly and put their heads together, whispering.

Sara's parents rushed to the table. Agnes stood, gaping, unable to speak. Horrified at the scene, her eyes went from John, who was lightly massaging his knuckles, to Chet, who began babbling incoherently from his prone position. After making sure Sara was all right, Joe also stared, speechless. Looking at Chet, he used a hand to shield the amused smirk spreading across his face.

John walked up to Sara.

"So, are you ready to leave?"

"I thought you'd never ask," Sara said, taking the arm he offered.

On the way home, Sara could not stop laughing.

"Did you see him?! Did you see the way he went down? People pay good money to see a fight like that. I swear, Mr. Olson, you do have a mean right hook. I didn't realize I was associating with a deadly weapon."

"Well, the poor guy was obviously victimized by your many charms before I ever got to him. You know, you've got quite an affect. I only hope that between the two of us, we didn't hurt him too badly."

"Oh, well, he had it coming. He's always been a pain. Gotten used to daddy helping him out, you know."

John nodded knowingly and then grew silent. Sara sensed a change in his mood.

"John, you've gotten quiet all of a sudden."

"Well, I guess some of the things Chet said were a bit troubling—if not true. What I mean to say is that I know I really don't fit in here. Never have. I'm just a horse of a different color."

"I know that, John. But who is to say these people are right? Most have been born with a silver spoon in their mouths. They've created their own private little worlds and little clique of friends and see no reason to look beyond. I think they're liars, actually. And what's worse is that they are lying to themselves—believing they're something they aren't."

"Still, I don't like to make trouble. I'll go back home, but you'll have to deal with the fallout after I'm gone."

"Oh, don't be silly. I can handle a buffoon like Chet. And who cares what they think, anyway. I'm glad you're here. I'm having a grand time—and this evenings raucous was especially exciting. As a matter of fact, I can't wait to see what you'll have up your sleeve for tomorrow."

"Maybe a sore hand," John said, smiling as he rubbed his knuckles.

John and Sara met downstairs the next morning early for breakfast. Joe and Agnes were still seated by the table, each reading a section of the newspaper. Joe greeted John brightly, but Agnes remained somewhat subdued, focusing her attention on the newsprint in front of her.

"So, John, what do you and Sara have planned for today?," Joe asked, pouring himself coffee from a nearby silver server.

"I couldn't say. Sara's been calling all the shots."

"Oh, really? Did she call the shot in the jaw you dealt Mr. Armstrong last night as well?," Agnes quickly retorted.

"Now mother, don't be unpleasant. He had it coming and John did an excellent job of putting him in his place. Hopefully he learned something from it and will think twice before shooting off his mouth in public," Sara shot back, irritated.

"So," Joe interjected, anxious to change the subject, "Sara, tell us what you've got planned for our guest."

"Go into the city again, I think. John didn't have a proper tour guide when he was stationed here during the war, and there's a lot he hasn't seen. And of course, I believe I heard Macy's is having a sale."

"Sorry, John," Joe said, patting his shoulder in mock-sympathy. Taking one last drink of his coffee, Joe stood up. "Well, I'd better be moving along." Pausing, he dropped a quick kiss on Sara's head. "Be easy on the poor guy, will you? We want him to say nice things about us when he gets back to Nebraska."

Agnes quickly picked up her husbands lead. Mumbling something about an appointment she hustled out of the room, leaving John and Sara to eat alone.

Although they waited to avoid the morning rush hour, traffic was again heavy. Using a different route to Manhattan, Sara decided to take the Lincoln Tunnel. John was shocked that such an underground roadway could be constructed. Moving through the near-darkness, a slight sense of claustrophobia began to envelope him. He was relieved to reach the tunnels end where the sunlight washed away the eerie, artificial darkness.

Again, Sara made her way to the same parking lot they had used earlier. Fortunately, one stall was available and she slid the car into it. Then, the two set off on foot to explore the city.

Although the traffic and number of people on Manhattan streets had been large for the Independence Day celebration, the weekday crowd was worse. Everyone seemed to be on a mission, sure of where they were headed and how to get there. Looking around, John thought he would never get used to a world of solid concrete. Regardless of where he looked, John could not find any sign of greenery. Not a tree or single blade of grass could be seen. John knew he was a long way from home.

"It's not exactly Nebraska," Sara said, reading his mind. "Maybe I can offer you a compromise."

Sara and John made a beeline for Central Park. There, a group of bicyclists were organizing for a ride through the park. Sara spotted a small stand where bicycles could be rented and got one for each of them. For several hours, the two made their way through the park. They took out time to look at the animals in the small zoo and feed the birds congregated around an enormous water fountain.

Eventually, they returned their bicycles. After lunch in a small cafe, Sara and John drifted into the Metropolitan Museum of Art. They spent the remainder of the day viewing the museum's many artifacts.

When they emerged, the sky was becoming dark. John glanced upwards, and it occurred to him that a New Yorker could go for weeks without actually seeing the sun. The passage of each day was marked under the shadow of sky scrapers.

John never realized how much he counted on the Nebraska sun. While it warmed the soil and oversaw the changing of seasons, it also provided him with a sense of direction. Morning and night were clearly distinct, keeping his life on a steady time table. There were morning chores, afternoon duties, and jobs that had to be completed before the sun disappeared into the west.

He could see why it would be easy for New Yorkers to lose track of time, causing day and night to blend into one. New York was the city that never slept, because nothing in the heavens tucked it in at night, or roused it with brimming hopefulness at days dawn.

Instead, the city stewed restlessly, its cacophony of harsh, artificial lights and metallic sounds coaxing a false sense of adrenalin. So its residents scurried, always in a hurry, always in search of an unattainable sense of peace.

Still, it was intriguing to be, for a change, in the center of things. Despite the city's many falsehoods, it sensed its power and influence and flaunted them unsparingly. New York was the place where things happened and to be in the midst of that pulsating fervor was exciting indeed.

Staying on main walkways, Sara and John made their way to Broadway. They enjoyed looking at the marquees and Sara filled John in on some of the plots. Hungry, Sara coaxed John into a small Chinese restaurant. John initially had reservations about the food, but decided to be a sport and give it a try. Although he finished his plate, he left thinking a good old-fashioned hamburger might have been a wiser choice.

On the way to their car, Sara veered off to the Palace Theater box office and plunked down money for an evening show. She handed them to John triumphantly.

"Here you go, Mr. Olson. A trip to New York wouldn't be complete without taking in a Broadway show!"

Walking back to the car, Sara suggested they get a cab. The Times Square area was less than desirable at any time of the day, and she wasn't prepared to have a confrontation.

Several minutes later they were sitting safely in Sara's car, heading out of the Manhattan borough.

During the next two days, John and Sara opted to stay around home. They visited at length, discussing their lives, opinions and views on many different subjects. Dunning swim suits, the two took advantage of the the Morris' outdoor swimming pool. For a treat, they strolled to a small convenience store located about a mile from the house. There, John bought them each an ice cream to enjoy.

In the evenings, Sara and John sat by the piano. Sara played and sang and occasionally John was able to accompany her. It was a relaxing time, which both took advantage of.

But before they went to bed, Sara decided it was time to give John fair warning about the upcoming day.

"Tomorrow, I think we should do something different. I have someplace I'd like to take you, but we've got to get an early start. So be prepared!"

John was intrigued by Sara's words, but decided not to press. He was grateful Sara had given him a couple of days to rest from his journey to New York. But now he was ready for adventure and felt up to Sara's challenge.

Before the sun was up the next morning, John was awakened by a tap on his door. Groggy, he made his way across the plush carpet to answer. He was surprised to see Sara standing there, fully dressed.

"Get up, sleepy head! We've got to get going!"

"Going? Didn't we just go to sleep?"

"Maybe, but you're going to be here only a few days, and I feel duty-bound to show you all the sights. So hurry and get dressed. We'll eat breakfast on the way."

John was ready a short time later. As soon as he reached the bottom of the stairs, Sara began pushing him toward the door.

"Why are we in such a hurry?," John asked, suspicious.

"Well, I thought it would be nice to beat the traffic. Besides, the action at Fulton's Fish Market takes place early."

"Fish Market?," John repeated, still not completely coherent.

"Come on, silly. Just get in the car."

Sara had packed sausage and egg sandwiches, juice and coffee and the trip into New York went quickly. Slipping into the city along the coastline, the borough seemed amazingly tranquil. But there seemed to be a lot of activity along the dock area. Sara found an empty parking spot and the two got out to look around.

The first thing John noticed was the smell. He had been up close and personal to cow manure for most of his life, but it was nothing compared to the overpowering odor of fish hanging in the air.

His attention was quickly diverted by the amount of activity taking place. Everywhere he looked yellow forklifts were busy shuffling around large crates. They were being loaded into trucks parked nearby.

As far as the eye could see, more crates were neatly set into place. All were full of fish in every imaginable color and shape. Shark, tuna, scallops and shrimp were all there. Beside some crates were buyers and sellers haggling over prices. One bristly-faced man dressed in a dirty, rumpled t-shirt cupped a pencil and notebook in his hand as he tried to convince a customer his catch was superior. The buyer, a small, olive-skinned Italian, shook his head from side to side in disagreement.

It was like a separate world, blind to the skyscrapers looming nearby. The place was surrounded with an energy John had not known existed in the city. These were hard-working, knowledgeable men who were used to getting their hands dirty to make a living. John guessed it was the closest thing to a Nebraska work ethic he would find in New York.

After about an hour of looking around, Sara and John headed south to catch a ferry for the Statue of Liberty. Sara hoped it would be early enough in the day to avoid the typically long wait.

Her hunch was right, although a line was already beginning to form, they managed to be in one of the first groups to travel to the top. After they reached Lady Liberty's head and took a few pictures they returned to the base and took a tour through the museum area.

Traveling back to the main island, they passed by Ellis Island. Back in Manhattan they had lunch in a nice restaurant. They spent the rest of the day sightseeing.

One of their last stops was Macy's, where John decided to splurge on a blazer set and new pair of shoes. He mentioned wistfully that it would be nice to wear it to the theater that evening.

"No problem," Sara shot back. "We can go to dad's office. He's got a private bathroom there."

So the two set off. Four blocks later the elevator was taking them up to the 32nd floor of a downtown hi-rise. When they got out, Sara made her way down a stark-white corridor flanked by several glass doors. Sara continued down the hall to a door that read "Morris and Associates" in stark gold letters.

She spoke briefly to a secretary who motioned her into an office. As if she'd done it many times, Sara made for the door, knocking briefly before entering.

"Hi, daddy. How are you?"

Mr. Morris was buried behind a stack of papers framed by a shiny oak desk. He stood up and hugged his daughter briefly.

"Hello, dear. Nice of you to stop by. Hello, John. Looks like you two have had a long day. Hope Sara hasn't been too hard on you."

"Not at all, Mr. Morris. Sara is a wonderful tour guide."

"Daddy, John was wondering if he could use your restroom to change. We're heading for a show after dinner."

"Of course, go right through that door, John. Now tell me, Sara, not to put a damper on your evening, but have you heard anything from the job prospects you've looked into?"

"Yes, as a matter of fact. There's a private elementary school here in Manhattan that's called me in for a second interview. I think I could easily get in."

"And..."

"Well, I just don't know. Frankly, the staff there didn't impress me much. They all seemed rather, well, catty, if you know what I mean."

"How about some of the business leads you've followed up on? I ran into Pete Armstrong yesterday. Said he's still interested in giving you a shot at his office."

126

"Chet's dad? After that little scene at the club? You've got to be kidding!"

"Well, I'll admit there's probably more to it than simply being enamored with your business knowledge. It wouldn't take much encouragement and you'd have young Chet at your beck and call."

"Well, wouldn't I be proud," Sara said, biting her lip to control her smile.

John entered the room, tugging at a price tag attached to his shirt sleeve.

"My, don't you look like a true New Yorker! Here, let me help you with that tag." Sara said, grabbing a pair of scissors out of her father's desk drawer.

"I'm pleased you're having an opportunity to see some of New York's offerings, John. Just remember, you can never be too cautious. There are a lot of people here, and it just takes one to spoil a perfectly grand time."

"Yes, sir. That's good advice. I'll be sure and keep it in mind," John said.

Sara moved toward John, slipping her arm through his.

"Well, Mr. Olson, we'd better be on our way. I made reservations at one of my favorite restaurants while we were out and about today. Oh, dad. Can you get John's clothes home O.K? We won't be going back to the car right now."

"Oh, yes. Fine. Fine. I'll see you both tomorrow."

Sara and John took the elevator downstairs and flagged a taxi. The evening began smoothly at the restaurant Sara chose. John was relieved to see a good deal of traditional, meat-and-potato style fare on the menu.

Afterwards, they made their way to the Palace Theater. Sara had pulled a few strings to reserve two prime seats. The musical production was John's first and he loved every minute of it. His only association with acting in North Platte had taken place at the high school, when seniors put on an annual play. Occasionally, a group of people from the community, in need of a creative fund raiser, would scrape up a few people with local talent and put on a one-time show.

Mrs. Ogstead was a master at planning such events. Involved in every social group in town, she prided herself on her ability to organize community events. Weighing in at around 200 pounds, she would flutter about in the bright, crisply ironed cotton dresses she was known for.

Her methods were well known by townspeople. First, a worthwhile cause would come to her attention. Although nothing formal would happen for a couple weeks, she would begin bringing it up at card meetings and church coffees.

"My," she would remark casually, her plump red cheeks squeezed by an animated smile, "Remember our last community play? Wasn't it grand? We should think about doing that again." Or, as she ran into Mr. George, owner of the corner market, she would pause and nonchalantly remark, "Mr. George, its a pity to let acting talent like yours go to waste. You were such a perfectly grand villain at our last production, I just heard someone remark on your performance again the other day. What do you say, Mr. George? Are you up to it again," she would chirp, fiddling with glittering gold clip on her handbag.

Eventually, through charm and perseverance, Mrs. Ogstead would get the towns business owners behind her. The lumber shop owner Mr. Gillman would be tap-tap-tapping away on a makeshift set in his spare time, and art students from the high school would be called in to put paint to wood. After about a month of rehearsals, the curtain would finally rise to the applause of town residents.

Then, the curtain would fall, everybody breathing a sigh of relief as they slapped each other on the back ceremoniously. As an afterthought, the cash box would be tallied and then tallied again in surprised disbelief. Eventually, the funds would be presented to Mrs Ogstead's needy cause, camera flash from the local newspaper capturing the effort for posterity. Then, the matter would be discreetly slid aside with hopes Mrs. Ogstead's charitable nature would diminish before another need tweaked her conscious again.

But the concept of being able to present the same show, over and over again for days and weeks amazed John. Furthermore, he'd never seen such elaborate sets and costumes. The production included a few lively dance numbers and the amount of practice necessary to perfect the carefully choreographed moves amazed the North Platte man.

They arrived home late that night, still caught up in the upbeat mood of the evening. Unlocking the front door, Sara and John entered, still talking and laughing about the evening. Making their way to the parlor, both were surprised to see Agnes Morris sitting in an easy chair and sipping a glass of wine.

"Mother, it's kind of late for you, isn't it?," Sara said, mild concern fleeting across her face.

"Well, it really wasn't so long ago that I was in your shoes. I think I can still handle a late night occasionally."

"Oh, I see," Sara said moving away from her mother and taking a seat across from her. John followed suit, sitting on a sofa facing the two.

"Of course," Agnes continued slowly, "I was probably a little more conscious of my actions than you are now."

"Are you saying I am unconscious of my actions?," Sara said, getting annoyed.

Agnes stared at her drink as she traced the smooth crystal rim with her finger. "I didn't say that, dear. But there have been a few interesting developments in the last few days which should give you pause."

"Mother, for heavens sake, what are you talking about? That Chet Armstrong incident? Because if you are..."

"No! Heavens no. I think we all know where I stand on that fiasco. No, it seems another matter has tongues wagging."

"I don't know if I want to hear this."

"Sara, you need to. And so does your guest, if he is at all concerned about how you look to your peers. It seems that the two of you are becoming quite an item. You've been seen all over town together. People are beginning to make some natural assumptions."

"Mother, for heavens sake. John is my — no, our — guest. I'm very happy to have him here and frankly I don't care what conclusions people draw. And let's be honest. It isn't my peers that you're worried about. It's that gossipy bunch of old cronies you hang around with that are bent on stirring up trouble for others that are the problem."

"None the less, those are the people with whom your father and I associate. They also happen to be some of the people who have a good deal to say about who makes it and who doesn't in this town. So if you hope to ever make an impression, perhaps you'd better remember exactly who it is you need to impress."

Sara leapt to her feet, her faced flushed with anger. John also arose, uncomfortable with the conversation he had unwittingly become a part of.

"Look, mother. New York is not the only place in the world. There are other places — places far away from here where people don't even care about New York, much less the few who your so bent on wowing."

"Well, dear, your perfectly free to investigate those places. However, since the doors are already open for you here, I wish you would just have a little consideration. I'm sure it would carry you a long way."

"Mother, you are completely exasperating. Please excuse us. But its been a long day and I'm really getting quite tired." Sara motioned to John with a quick nod, and the two headed out of the room.

"Sorry about that," Sara said. "Nobody ever accused my mother of keeping her opinions to herself. At least not where I'm concerned, anyway. I hope you don't pay any attention to what she said. Mother is always overreacting to one thing or another. You have to just take her with a grain of salt."

"I understand," John said, not really sure he understood at all. "Well, like you said, it is late and I suppose I'd better get some shuteye."

"O.K. We'll see you in the morning, then. Good night."

"Good night," John said, disappearing behind his bedroom door.

Although he hadn't let on, John found he was very upset by Agnes' words. Was it true? Was his presence in New York compromising Sara's reputation and narrowing her job possibilities?

Laying in his bed, John mulled the questions over in his mind. There was no doubt he cared about Sara and wanted to save her from embarrassment at all cost. And if he was a problem, there was only one thing to do.

The next morning, John found Sara sitting in the breakfast nook as usual. He took a seat across from her and began to disinterestedly flip through the daily paper.

"Good morning, John. Sleep well?," Sara asked, peering over the top of a glass of orange juice as she lifted it to her lips.

"Well, actually, I had a hard time getting to sleep."

"Don't tell me my mother managed to get to you. Really, you shouldn't think about it twice. It's just her nature to be troublesome."

"No, Sara. I have a good deal of respect for your mother and what she thinks. Frankly, if she thought this important enough to bring to your attention, there's probably something behind it."

"John, what are you saying, exactly?"

"Sara, I think its time for me to go. I was beginning to worry about things back home anyway."

"But, you had planned on a few more days. Who knows when, or even if you'll ever make it out this way again. Besides, I'll miss you. You have a way of growing on a person, you know," Sara smiled, popping a piece of fruit into her mouth.

John smiled back admiring how the morning sun glistened on Sara's hair and formed a glowing halo. It was hard to remain somber around her for long.

"Well, the feeling is mutual. But I'm sure there will be another time."

Sara stared down at her plate sullenly, deep in thought. After a time, she looked at John and shot him a downcast smirk.

"I guess my visit to North Platte ended with a run-in with a prairie wolf and your visit to New York ended with a run-in with my mother. It seems a bit ironic, wouldn't you say?"

John chuckled, getting to his feet.

"If you don't mind, I'd like to use your phone and check on train departure times."

"Oh, yes, yes. Of course. Please go right ahead," Sara said.

As John turned to leave the room, Joe entered the room.

"What's this I hear about train departures?," he said.

"Good morning, Mr. Morris. I thought you had left for the office and was planning to drop by and tell you goodbye. It looks as if the time for me to head back home has arrived. But I did want to thank you for your hospitality. It was very nice of you to open your home to me as you have and its been a pleasure getting to know you."

"As it was you, John. But I thought your stay with us was to last a few days more. I hope you aren't leaving on our account."

"Not at all. But I have obligations in Nebraska that I've put on hold and should get back to."

"John, your an A-1 young man," Joe said, extending his hand. If you come out this way again, please let us know."

"Thank you, Mr. Morris. Now, if you'll excuse me, I need to make a few phone calls."

As John left the room, Joe looked at Sara questioningly. From her pursed lips and strumming fingers, he quickly filled in the blanks.

The ride to Grand Central station was mostly silent. Sara's disappointment and anger with her mother simmered just below the surface.

"How dare mother provoke John to leave like this," she fumed silently. "Such a fine man and she can't even look beyond herself to see him for who he is."

John, aware Sara was upset, tried to think of something to say that would ease the tension. But he had to admit that he, too, was unhappy to be leaving. Trying to think of something positive to say in light of the situation was a difficult task.

"Sara, before we get to the station, I just want to tell you I had a really wonderful time. I never got to enjoy New York as I have with you these last few days. And you were a great hostess. I'm sure I'll always remember my time here with you fondly."

"Well, it's nothing like Nebraska, but New York does have some good points. Just remember, if you ever travel up this way again, I expect you to give me a call."

Sara was lucky enough to find a parking near the terminal and hastily slipped her car into a spot. The two walked slowly, side by side, to John's train.

The irony was not lost to John.

"You know, in the short time we've known each other, it seems like we're always saying goodbye. And here we are again."

"Yes, I know what you mean. But we'll speak again soon. I'll be settling on a job soon and I'll give you a call to let you know my new address."

"I'll be waiting. Good luck until then."

John grabbed up his bags. "Well, I guess this is where I say goodbye. Take care, Sara." Without hesitating, he dipped down and gave Sara a quick kiss on the cheek. With a smile, he turned on his heel and disappeared up the train's steps.

Sara was warmed by John's farewell, and searched for a glimpse of him before he left. As the train lurched forward, she saw him waving from an aisle seat and frantically gestured back.

The terminal was crowded, but Sara took her time leaving the station. Reaching her car, she got in and slowly maneuvered it out of the downtown area. On the way home, she took a familiar exit and headed for a wooded area where her father occasionally went hunting.

Pulling into a special parking area, Sara killed the motor but remained sitting in the car. She knew she was overly upset and emotional. Yet, she could not reason her feelings into submission.

"Mother had absolutely no right to talk to me like that when John was right there. It was unconscionable. And all she did was make hard feelings."

Sara sat for a long time, stewing, her feelings of anger continuing to grow.

"It's as though mother thinks she can live my life for me. But she can't. I need to start running my own life . Either that, or face being married to Chet Armstrong — or someone just like him. And that, mother dear, is not likely to happen."

Starting the car, Sara jammed it into reverse and then drive, shooting onto a nearby gravel road. Speeding homeward, a trail of dust chased her across the countryside.

When Sara arrived home, Agnes was in the foyer arranging flowers in a vase. Sara greeted her icily, quickly pushing past her towards the study. Ruffling through a folder of applications, she came across what she was looking for and quickly extracted it from the pile.

Taking a seat in her fathers plush leather desk side chair, Sara carefully dialed the phone.

A few minutes later, the voice of a cheerful secretary filled the phone line.

"Hello, North Platte Elementary school, can I help you?"

Sara hesitated for just a moment before answering.

"Yes, this is Sara Morris. I would like to speak with the principal, please."

Chapter 8

For Sara, the next few days were a blur.

She'd spoken with the North Platte principal for just a few minutes, but as she hung up the phone her hand was shaking visibly. It seemed horribly wrong. It seemed deliciously right. But the sense of relief that flooded Sara as she accepted the North Platte teaching job was unmistakable.

She'd been in a daze after the phone call, simultaneously euphoric, yet mortified by her own boldness. Anyone who knew Sara knew she was strong-willed and often spontaneous. But no one knew better than her the ramifications of her decision.

The first matter of business was to inform her parents, which she promptly did. For Sara, their reaction was somewhat predictable. Joe shook his head in dismay, but said little. His reaction was overshadowed by Agnes' mortified response. From her spot upon the parlor settee, she first let out a yelp of horror. Grabbing her chest, she repeated "My God, I can't believe it. Sara, surely you can't be serious." Each time, Agnes sank farther and farther into the chair until she felt as though she was being swallowed up..

The scene continued for several minutes, with Agnes becoming increasingly incensed. "Sara, how could you even think of doing this to your father and I. After all we've done to open doors for you here," she ranted.

Finally, Joe could take it no more. Rising to his feet, he glared angrily at his wife as Sara looked on.

"Agnes, for heavens sake, stop trying to run our daughters life. You act as if you're the one going to live in North Platte. If your going to miss Sara, then tell her. Otherwise, please get hold of yourself and stop acting like this is the end of the world."

Agnes and Sara sat, stunned. Neither mother or daughter had ever heard Joe speak out in such a manner before. Sara looked at him wide-eyed, snapping to her senses when she realized her mouth was hanging open in shock. But Agnes reacted more quickly and began sobbing loudly. Dismayed, Joe left the room in silence.

So it had gone for the next several days. Sara noticed her parents were barely on speaking terms. Meals together were a chilly affair, with only the tinkle of spoon against China breaking the silence. Afterwards, the three Morris' would go their separate ways with barely a word.

Sara was distraught over her parents reaction and even feared for their future together. But she had made a decision and needed to follow through.

The first order of business would be to find an apartment. The principal had given Sara a list of places that might have openings. She set to work almost immediately contacting the owners.

After narrowing down the possibilities, Sara decided it would be a good idea to plan the move to Nebraska as soon as possible. She thought it would be nice to get settled in before the school year began.

With hopes of enlisting the help of her father, Sara approached him cautiously one day after dinner.

"So," she hedged, "It looks like you and mom are against my decision."

Legs crossed in the comfortable arm chair in which he sat, Joe chuckled lightly.

"Oh, I wouldn't say I'm against it, exactly. Of course, I'm worried about my little girl going so far away from home. It will be hard on both your mother and me not to see you regularly. But, you've just signed a one-year contract. I'm sure we can all last that long. And then, if you don't like it, you can always come back to New York, write a thesis on your experience as a Nebraska grade school teacher, and apply it to a graduate degree. And the hell with it."

"So, you don't mind me giving this a try?"

"No. We all have to go out and make our own decisions. But I am wondering just how much of this has to do with John Olson. Is there more going on between the two of you than I know?"

Sara thought about her answer carefully before answering.

"No, dad. Actually, there isn't. John is just a very good friend I really enjoy spending time with. And I'm grateful he was able to open up this door for me. But my decision has more to do with wanting to try something on my own. I really appreciate all you and mom have done for me — all the educational opportunities, chances to socialize and work with people in a variety of professions. But frankly, I just want to see if I can succeed on my own."

Joe was silent, rubbing his chin thoughtfully. He reflected on his own youth and recalled the excitement and anticipation of those early days. It had been such a confusing, yet hopeful time. With the energy of youth, it had been his time to strike out. And he realized that it was the same for his lovely, spirited daughter.

"Yes, I guess I can see your point. Now is the time to try something new in your life," Joe said.

Sara smiled, relieved by her father's support.

"So, what's your plan?," Joe asked.

"Funny you should ask," Sara said, her smile broadening. "How would you like to take a little drive. To Nebraska."

"Actually, that doesn't sound half bad. We could make a little sight-seeing trip of it. But I have to warn you, I have a feeling your mother won't go for it. It will take her a while to adjust."

"Yes, I gathered as much. So when do you think you can get away?"

"Let's try the first week in August. That should give us plenty of time."

With that, it was settled. Sara spent the next couple weeks getting her affairs in order and packing what she needed for what would be her most lengthy stay yet in Nebraska.

One evening, Sara decided it was time check in with John. Picking up the phone, she was gripped momentarily with apprehension. Setting the phone back on the receiver, Sara tried to get a grip on her feelings.

It had only been a few weeks since she last saw John, but to her it seemed like years had passed. So much had happened since they last spoke. And while John always seemed opened to new ideas, it suddenly occurred to Sara that he had no way of foreseeing this turn of events. What would he think? John didn't even know Sara had interviewed for the North Platte teaching position. Would he read her finding a position there the wrong way?

Sara hadn't considered any of these questions. Walking away from the phone, she decided it would be better to give John the news later.

After about a week, Sara again found herself staring at the telephone in her father's study. She had resolved none of the questions that disturbed her earlier, but time was growing short. She and her father were scheduled to leave in just three days.

Picking up the phone, she dialed quickly but then hung up. Angry with herself, she dialed again and listened to the phone ring on the other end. A familiar voice answered.

"Hello, this is Helen."

"H-Hello, Helen, this is Sara," she said, speaking evenly. "How are you?"

"Why, Sara! What a pleasure to hear your voice again! We are all just fine. And you?"

"Oh, very well."

"That's good, dear. Now, I know better than to think you called to chat with me. Let me see if I can track that son of mine down. Just a minute."

The phone went dead on the other end for what seemed like several minutes. Finally, Sara heard the unmistakable sound of the screen door opening and closing.

"Hello?"

"Hello, John. Did I call at a bad time?"

"No! Not at all. My, this is a surprise. It's nice to hear your voice."

"Well, I told you I'd call when I got a job."

"You got a job already? You must have been busy with interviews."

"Yes, it looks like I'll be a fifth grade teacher. I signed a year contract."

"That's sounds good. Let's see. I'll get a pencil and paper to get your new address."

"Oh, that's O.K. I don't think you'll have any problem remembering it."

"Oh?"

"Well, I haven't actually found an apartment yet. But I know the city and state."

"O.K., shoot."

"Well, North Platte. North Platte, Nebraska."

John stood holding the phone, stunned.

"Are you serious? How did you manage that?"

"Well, its kind of a long story. But dad and I will be leaving here in about three days. I wanted plenty of time to get my things in order before school started."

"That's ...great!," John said, still stunned. "But I don't understand. Why Nebraska? Wouldn't you have felt more comfortable getting a job closer to home?"

"I looked. But for some reason, nothing seemed appealing. It's kind of like a fresh start for me. What I accomplish will be on my own merit. Fortunately, my parents influence doesn't extend as far as Nebraska."

John was silent a moment, trying to absorb everything Sara said. Her actions seemed encoded, holding a hidden meaning. It was not like her to make a hasty, unplanned decision. Yet to John, this seemed to be exactly what Sara was doing.

"John, are you still there?"

"Yes! Oh, I'm sorry, I got distracted for a minute. Why, that's wonderful! I'm glad to hear you'll be coming here. Will you need any help moving in?"

"No, it's nice of you to offer, but I think dad and I will have it covered."

"All right, then. I look forward to seeing you after you arrive."

As Sara hung up, she was wracked with a feeling of confusion. She knew there was a reason she'd been putting off calling John, but his reaction wasn't what she expected. She had hoped he would be happy about her relocation, but his response seemed reserved. What did he know that she didn't? Was she making a choice she would regret later?

Sara's brief visit with John was a reality check and she dwelled on it for the next few days. Even as she packed her belongings into her father's near-new 1949 Chrysler, doubts crowded her mind. She remained subdued as she told her mother goodbye—a chilly affair that ended with Agnes wiping a few tears from her eye.

The first part of their journey westward was mostly silent. Sara reflected on her decision solemnly. A couple of times, she was almost ready to call it quits, tell her father to return home, and forget this foolish idea of striking out on her own.

But each time, the urge died on her lips. Sara knew she couldn't back out. She had taken too great a risk to get to this point, and she wasn't willing to give up without a fight now.

Yet, she wished to get some insight on what her future might hold. As the miles melted away, Sara approached the subject with her father.

"Dad, do you think I'm doing the wrong thing?"

Joe pursed his lips together, then spoke thoughtfully.

"Neither of us know how this thing will work out. That's the way it is in life. We make decisions and hope for the best. But your still young and have a lot of opportunities open to you if this falls through. Just remember you can always come home if you need to."

Joe's words seemed to put the whole thing into perspective for Sara, and she was finally able to relax. After that, their conversation seemed to flow easily. Father and daughter shared their views on a variety of subjects, laughing together often.

They stopped at a roadside motel, and got an early start the next day. After lunch, they crossed the Nebraska border. As they left Omaha behind, the roadside became less and less populated. Gradually, corn fields gave way to prairie land and cattle outnumbered people. Joe was surprised, unprepared for the areas isolation.

The flat, steady road gave way to miles of unbroken countryside. As they made their way to the eastern edge of the sandhills, Sara and Joe were lulled by the areas quiet beauty. The car hummed steadily beneath them, creating a steady, predictable rhythm.

Suddenly, the Morris' tranquility was shattered. From the car's rear, a large BOOM rang out. Joe had a difficult time steering the car, which ground to a quick stop at the side of the road.

Joe and Sara got out to survey the situation. A rear tire had blown out, leaving nothing but a helpless tangle of rubber around the rim. Joe bent down to survey the damage, then set to work emptying out the trunk to get to the spare tire below.

Sara had packed a good deal into the back of the car, and within a short time it was all in a pile on the road. Initially, Mr. Morris had a difficult time trying to find a spot to attach the jack. When he did finally get the car up, he struggled to loosen the bolts. Twice, the wrench slipped causing Joe to scuff his hand. Pushing down hard a third time he realized the nuts would not move.

Huffing and puffing, he and Sara sat on the car's running board. Mr. Morris looked one way, and then another, scanning the landscape. No form of life could be seen in any direction.

Suddenly, with a twinkle in his eye, he turned to his daughter.

"What on earth have we gotten ourselves into? If only your mother could see us now," he said, smiling wryly.

Amused by the look on his face, Sara giggled, than began laughing hardily. Realizing how humorous the situation was, Joe joined in — chuckling softly at first, but then more loudly. Their laughter grew until both were holding their stomachs.

Eventually, they sobered, still unsure of what to do next. In the distance, Sara spotted a truck coming their way, and excitedly motioned to her father. Drawing near, the pickup slowed and a middle-aged man wearing a cowboy hat stuck his head out an open window to survey the situation.

"You look like you need some help," the cowboy said.

"Yes," Mr. Morris replied, "badly."

The rancher jumped out of his pickup and looked the situation over. Going back to his vehicle, he got a small can of oil and dabbed it on the stubborn nuts.

"You'll be on your way in a jiffy," the good Samaritan said.

The man slipped on the tire wrench and coaxed the bolts loose with minimal effort. In less then fifteen minutes, the new tire was on and the threesome began repacking suitcases into the trunk.

"We can't thank you enough," Mr. Morris said, impressed by the mans kindness. "How much do we owe you for your trouble."

"Oh, that's O.K. Maybe you'll be able to help out somebody that needs it sometime."

With that, the man said his goodbyes and sped off. After packing a few more things, Joe and Sara slammed down the trunk lid and were on their way, as well.

After reaching North Platte, Sara located a pay phone and started calling the apartment owners she'd made contact with earlier. She and her father went to see three different apartments before settling on a furnished one located just three blocks away from the school.

The pair hastily carried in Sara's belongings, then headed for the local grocery store to make sure her pantry was well stocked. To celebrate her arrival, father and daughter enjoyed a supper of fried hamburgers cooked in Sara's new kitchen.

Joe spent the night camped out on Sara's couch. After breakfast, he announced that he must be heading back to New York.

"Oh, and by the way, I'll be taking the train."

"What? I thought you'd be driving back."

"No. Living way out here, you're going to need some transportation. Just keep the car. Maybe we'll switch and you can get yours back some day. Just take care of old Bessie," Joe said, joking.

Sara gave her father a hug and teary-eyed kiss. Then the two left for the train depot. She waved frantically as the iron beast swung into motion, carrying her father back to New York. For a long time she continued to stand there, alone for the first time.

***

The first weeks of school flew by. Sara found the students in her class delightful. They were open to learning and lacked the haughty attitude so prevalent in many private New York schools she had visited. While they could tell from Sara's brogue that she was different, they seemed to have no trouble accepting her. And she was amazed that they, too, had much to offer. The North Platte students had a whole array of interests that were completely new to Sara. They offered her a different way of looking at the world. Sara found their positive attitudes made her anxious to wake up and go to work each morning.

She also quickly made friends with several staff members. One, named Dagmar, had also recently moved into the area. She, however, was a west coast native. During lunch break, she filled Sara in, telling her how she'd initially come out to visit her aunt and uncle on a nearby ranch for the summer. On a whim, she decided to stay and the rest "was history" as she was so fond of saying.

On the weekends, Sara had a standing date with John. While they sometimes went out, they often found themselves sitting in Sara's apartment or the Olson's living room, exchanging stories about their week. They discovered it really wasn't necessary for them to go out to have a good time together.

Sara's spirits remained high, buoyed up by her new-found sense of independence. She discovered she liked making her own money and being responsible for her own expenses. It offered a sense of control she'd never known before.

But as the leaves began to fall and the trees sat bare and naked under gray skies, Sara's thoughts were drawn to New York. She remembered that day, so long ago, when she walked across her college campus and reflected on her future. Fall was often the time new Broadway plays got kicked off and designers flaunted their newest styles.

Conversations with her parents did little to ease growing feelings of homesickness. Her mother still only spoke to her briefly, and then it was with a guilt-laden undercurrent. And her father, wrapped up in business matters, knew little about the latest tidbits of information that would have interested his daughter.

To compensate, Sara threw herself into her work. But putting in long hours just made her more tired and depressed. Soon, her students and co-workers began noticing her subdued demeanor.

141

November brought the first dusting of snow to Nebraska. Students in Sara's class began preparing for their annual Christmas play and families began making plans for the Thanksgiving holiday.

For the first time, Sara began missing her family. For as long as she could remember, she had always been with her parents during the holidays. But, because of her mothers negative attitude and the short amount of time allowed for Thanksgiving vacation, Sara knew she wouldn't be making it home. The knowledge only seemed to bring her spirits down more.

Dagmar, who had gone through similar emotions after moving to Nebraska, sympathized with Sara. After school one day, she came into her classroom and handed her a sheet of paper.

"Here's something you might be interested in," she said, taking a seat in a students desk.

"What's this? A horse club? I had no idea North Platte had something like this."

"I didn't either when I first moved here. But we do have a lot of fun. We try to go out weekly as a group. There's a stable north of here where you can rent a horse. We take them on a trail about two miles out of town."

"This sounds like fun. My parents own a stable back home, and I've always enjoyed riding. Tell you what. Count me in."

"Great. We meet at the stable after school on Fridays. See you there."

As promised, the group of teachers gathered together after school at the end of the week. They set off towards the stable, where each had their own horses reserved. Since Sara was new, the stable owner set her up with a spirited, dark brown mare.

However, as soon as the stable doors opened, Sara sensed her horse was uncomfortable. It acted flighty and seemed spooked by the slightest motion. Sara quickly dismounted and checked to make sure the horse was saddled correctly. Going to its head, she stroked its nose gently and spoke to it in a quiet, soothing voice. Then, Sara walked around the animal, stroking it and examining it for problems.

The stable owner chuckled at Sara's reaction.

"Looks like you aren't used to riding," he said, a piece of straw hanging out the corner of his mouth.

"Actually, I am. Are you sure this horse is used to being ridden? She seems a little jumpy."

"Yep. We put the little kids on that one. The only other ones available are a couple young stallions. Doubt you'd like either of them if this timid one's got you scared."

Sara didn't like the stableman's tone. However, the group was already saddled and waiting, so she felt she had no choice but to catch up. Mounting smoothly, the horse immediately began trotting forward.

The ride seemed to be going well. The club started riding on an open field that stretched for about a mile. Then, they got on a trail that wound around a stream.

The route had several trees with gracefully reaching branches. Sara thought they would be excellent to hang tire swings from. But her thoughts were broken when her horse veered under the lowest branch. Ducking quickly, Sara just avoided being knocked off.

Sara soon discovered her horse had a habit of passing beneath the lowest-hanging branches. Although she would tug on the reins, the stubborn animal continued to do as it liked.

The other riders teased Sara good-naturedly about her "well mannered" steed. Sara played along, all the while fighting the reins and ducking beneath branches. Eventually, she fell to the back of the line.

Without warning, the horse sped its pace. Before Sara realized what would happen, another low-lying branch appeared. Unable to react quickly enough, it hit Sara squarely in the head. As if awaiting its cue, the horse reared up slightly throwing its dazed rider onto the ground.

All of the other riders immediately stopped. Sara tried to get up, but a stabbing pain shot though her leg when she applied pressure. Dagmar, who had been keeping an eye on Sara, came to her side. Concern etched her forehead as she saw Sara's ankle begin turning blue.

"Looks like this is the last ride you'll be having for awhile," she said.

Another rider lifted Sara up on Dagmar's horse and the two set off back toward the stable. It was a harrowing ride for Sara, whose head and leg throbbed with each step the horse took.

At the hospital some time later, the doctor informed Sara that she had a broken ankle. She would be wearing a cast for the next six weeks.

When Sara finally got home, she was weary and downhearted.

"So this is what I get in Nebraska. A broken leg," she moaned.

Some time later, John arrived for their weekly date. He was surprised to find Sara laying on the couch with her leg propped on pillows and face wet with tears.

Between hiccuping sobs she told John what had happened.

"Oh John, I just don't think I did the right thing coming out here. But I can't admit it to my parents. Dad would just tell me to stick it out and mother would say 'I told you so.'" Sara's shoulders shook with sobs again. "I'm just so confused," she said, dabbing at her eyes daintily with a tissue.

John pulled up a chair and sat down. He had never seen Sara so downhearted, and was surprised at how deeply it saddened him. Without realizing it, he had become used to Sara's cheerful attitude bringing up his spirits. Seeing her so disheartened suddenly made him realize what an important influence this pretty young New Yorker had on his life.

Reaching out, John took Sara's hand in his.

"Sara, it's not so bad. I know you miss your family and friends in New York, but just look at all the friends you've made since you've moved here. And your students! They absolutely adore you. I overheard two mothers talking in the hardware store about you earlier this week. They both have students in your class, and they were saying how much their kids look forward to going to school each day. That's because of you, Sara."

Sara continued to sniffle, but listened in interest. It seemed John always had that effect on her. There was something about his voice that put everything into perspective. He never seemed to get rattled by things going on around him. Instead, he took what life had to offer in stride. Sara took great comfort in his ability.

"Yes, I guess you're right. It's just that, well, it was all just a lot at once, I guess. Acting like a grown-up when your not quite sure you are one can be confusing.

"But really, John, I just don't know where to go from here. I feel so out of place yet."

"Well, instead of looking back, why don't you concentrate on looking forward? What's the next big thing coming up at school?"

Sara's watery eyes suddenly dissolved into a tearful grin. Chuckling softly, she wiped her nose with a tissue.

"You're never going to believe this. On Monday, I'm supposed to give a speech to the whole student body and staff. And get this, the presentation is entitled 'Safety First.' Can you believe it? I'll have to wobble on stage with crutches and tell them how NOT to end up like me!"

Sara's giggle turned into a full-bellied laugh, and John, grateful to see her spirits rising, joined in. Eventually, their gales of laughter faded and a comfortable silence enveloped them. John once again took Sara's hand in his and spoke in a quiet tone.

"You know, I do hope you decide to stay. Life just wouldn't be the same without you."

Sara looked at John straight on and smiled widely.

"Why, Mr. Olson. That sounds like a compliment."

The next Monday morning, Sara readied herself to go on-stage for her presentation. When her name was announced, she made her way up the short flight of stairs with her crutches and sheepishly took her spot behind the podium. As she was about to begin speaking, a spattering of applause could be heard in the audience. Others picked up on the cue, and soon the whole auditorium shook with enthusiastic applause.

It was then that Sara realized she was indeed at home.

***

Mrs. Olson called Sara and invited her to spend Thanksgiving with them. She eagerly accepted, grateful not to be alone.

Sara had become more and more aware of the distance between her mother and herself. Since moving to Nebraska, Sara had only spoken to Agnes briefly over the phone and then it was uncomfortable. It seemed as if her mother was determined to win the battle.

But the day of Sara's horse-riding accident had been a turning point. Thanks to the support of John and her fellow teachers, the New Yorker was becoming more self-confident about her decision and ability to make her experience in Nebraska work out. And while she still missed her parents, it seemed to Sara they were a part of her past — a world she was no longer really a part of.

Sara tried to help out with the Thanksgiving meal as much as possible, but discovered it difficult to maneuver with the crutches. In the end, Helen shooed her from the kitchen, calling in Ed to assist.

When the dishes were cleared away, John and Ed went outside to do chores and feed the cattle. Helen and Sara were left to visit in the house.Sara had come to enjoy her talks with Helen, especially since her own mother was increasingly aloof.

The two settled onto the couch. After a while, Helen's voice took on a motherly tone.

"It must be hard for you, being away from your family like this."

"Well, the feelings of homesickness come and go. It is getting easier, though," Sara said, averting her eyes to hide her fib.

"You know, I know a little bit about this subject. My mother used to tell me stories about how difficult it was for them when them moved to the United States. You see, my family were immigrants here, farmers from a place near Lillihammer, Norway. When my parents were in their early 20's, they immigrated to Westby, Wisconsin with hopes of having a better life.

"But for dad, homesickness took over, and about a year after arriving they returned to Norway. But mother liked it here, and a year or so later they returned to Wisconsin. They farmed there, and later moved to Nebraska where they spent the remainder of their lives.

Helen continued, "My mother used to tell me how, on one hand, she missed the old country, but on the other hand, had longed to return to Wisconsin. Homesickness was such a factor in their decisions.

"You must have similar feelings as they. In the end, only you will know what to do. Just as they did."

Sara turned over Helen's words in her mind. Yes, moving to Nebraska had been like moving to a new country. She could see such transitions were never easy for the people involved. Like those early pioneers, she would have to decide what she wanted in life and follow her dream.

As John broke a bale for the cattle outside, he gazed into the distance and became lost in thought. It seemed as if Sara was always on his mind. Still, he didn't know if letting his feelings show would be wise. There was no doubt the move to Nebraska had been hard. And while he liked to think her decision to come west had something to do with him, John worried Sara may have simply made the move to spite her mother.

Letting Sara know about his growing feelings for her could chase her off. Or making a commitment could well mean he would one day have to leave the ranch in order to make her happy.

Would he be willing to give up the life he knew for Sara? John knew such a decision wouldn't be easy. His parents would then be alone. In addition, he would be leaving behind an occupation he loved. Yes, ranching had long hours and a good deal of headaches, but the land had provided him with a decent living.

Yet, he had a hard time envisioning life without Sara. She added color to the palate of his otherwise mundane existence. Yes, leaving the ranch would be hard. But living without Sara would be harder.

For now, at least, John decided he would wait. And if the time became right, he would let his heart have the last word.

The weeks of winter slipped by quickly. Sara tried to call home a few times, but Merle the butler was usually the only one in and nobody seemed interested in returning her phone calls. Finally, as the Christmas holiday drew close, Sara decided to contact her father at work.

"Dad?," Sara said, relieved to hear his voice, "Hi. It's me. I've begun to wonder about you all. I've left several messages at the house, but nobody's called back."

"Good to hear from you! Actually, I never got any notes you called. I'll have to ask your mother if she's been ambushing my messages. At any rate, I suspected things were going smoothly and you didn't have time to call."

"I was wondering what I should do for Christmas," Sara said, biting her lip nervously.

"Well, to be quite honest, your mother's been pretty negative lately. I think you'd better count her out of your holiday plans. At any rate, I don't think she'd be up for a trip to Nebraska. If you'd like to come home, however, it's up to you."

Sara mulled over her fathers words carefully.

"Well, Christmas is only two weeks away. Maybe it would be better for everyone if I just stayed here this year. I'll miss you. But it just might be easier all around."

After hanging up the phone, a sense of loss flooded over Sara. It seemed so unfair. Had she simply been a pawn in her mother's social climb? Why couldn't she be accepted for who she was? Sara struggled with the questions at length, falling into a greater and greater melancholy.

But while the relationship with her mother spiraled downward, Sara's relationship with John seemed to strengthen. He became her confidant and steadfast support. Sara realized that she was becoming increasingly reliant on him.

The Olson's invited Sara to spend the Christmas holiday with them. Although she had said nothing, she had been secretly hoping for the offer. True, it appeared a far better idea than spending the holiday alone in her own small apartment. But in truth, Sara had to admit that she was becoming increasingly attached to the Olson's. Helen, Ed and John had become like a second family. Sara chuckled as she thought about this more. The irony was, right now she was actually closer to Helen and Ed than her own parents.

As Christmas drew near, Sara discovered holiday festivities didn't last only one day as they did in the Morris home. The weekend before Christmas, Helen invited Sara over for, as Helen put it, "a taste of Norwegian customs." The pair started mixing cookie ingredients early one Saturday morning. By evening, more than 14 different types of cookies were spread throughout the Olson kitchen.

As the last cookie sheet was washed, dried, and put away, Sara collapsed into a kitchen chair. Every available surface in the tidy, warm kitchen held containers of freshly-baked cookies. In all her life, Sara had never been part of such a slow and time-consuming process. Yet, she and Helen had passed the time visiting and every so often John or Ed would pop in and grab a handful of the still-warm creations. As they sampled the days efforts, the men would sit down, warm their hands on a cup of fresh, steaming coffee and join in on Sara and Helen's banter.

Rubbing her feet, Sara asked Helen what she intended to do with all the bakery.

"My dear, come back tomorrow and you will see," she answered.

Sara did return to the Olson's after attending church the next day. Helen produced several colorful Christmas containers, and the two began filling them with the cookies. Agnes then ordered Ed to bring the car to the front of the house.

"Time to start making deliveries," she said, wiping her hands on her apron and then untying the bow.

Then Sara and Agnes drove from neighbor to neighbor delivering their sweet morsels. In most cases, Sara was surprised to see the neighbors prepared with special gift baskets to give in return.

As the day went on, Sara began to enjoy the experience more and more. Whether Helen knew it or not, she was giving Sara an opportunity to meet many new people in the area. And Sara loved the chance to get a peek in their homes and observe the customs of others — ranchers style.

On Christmas Eve, John picked Sara up at her apartment and brought her out early in the afternoon. The two rode horses out into a pasture, where John told Sara it was her job to pick the best-looking cedar tree she could. After trudging through the six-inch snow for about half a mile, Sara spotted one that looked about right. John promptly cut it off, tied it atop a makeshift sled he had hooked up behind his horse, and headed for home.

However, when John and Sara tried to set the tree upright in the Olson's living room, Sara realized she'd misjudged the tree's height. It ended up being a good three-feet taller than the ceiling.

By then, Helen appeared and took a seat on a nearby easy chair to watch the fun. Sara and John retraced their steps, yanking the tree through the door and outside once again.

John used a saw to recut the bottom of the tree, then returned to the house once again with Sara lifting the trees crown to avoid damage. But as they tried to put the tree into a bucket of water, they discovered that the tree was still too tall to manage.

Ed had entered the room and began coaching the duo on how to slide the tree into the bucket sideways. Sara held the bucket at an angel as John tipped the tree over and attempted to slide it in.

John was just about to claim victory, when the toe of his boot accidentally caught the leg of a small hassock. Losing his footing, he stumbled backward unexpectantly. As if seeing an advantage, the heavy, awkward cedar chased him downward. Before anybody in the room realized what had happened, John was laying on the floor, the Christmas tree blanketing him with sharp, fragrant needles.

"Help! The tree is winning!," John wailed as laughter rose in the room.

Eventually, the tree was lifted off John and propped up dutifully in a corner of the room. Helen brought a box of hand-made wooden ornaments down from the attic and Sara and John took charge of decorating the tree.

After the sun slid from the sky and left the area in a cold blanket of darkness, the Olsons and Sara went to the small country church where John was baptized.

With Sara's hand resting on his arm, John eyed the old church that had played such an important part in his life for so many years. It sat there, so humble and so different from the ornate chapels Sara must have attended with her family in New York.

Was it just one year ago that he gazed up at this church, a sense of wonder and promise welling in his breast? John considered the past year, and the turn of events that had conspired to shape his life since.

Sliding into a pew in the old familiar church, John gazed thoughtfully at the altar. A year ago, he would have never imagined being involved with a girl from New York. Yet, she was there, sitting beside him, unaware of fates role.

Looking deep into his heart, John wondered what God saw in him to inspire such a turn of events. A flood of gratitude washed over him as he contemplated his many gifts and opportunities for happiness. In the small country church that he had known all his life, surrounded by family and friends, John felt singled out. The favors dealt to him made him feel special in God's eyes, though unworthy of such divine intervention.

As the service progressed, John felt he was becoming more focused on the future than he ever had before. As his thoughts reached forward, each image that played through his mind consisted of one constant — Sara.

Her laughter, curiosity, intelligence and honesty carried the melody his visions danced to. He clung to the promise Sara's dance inspired and could not imagine the comfort of her sweet serenade coming to an end in his life.

Leaving the church on the wee hours of a new Christmas Day, John knew what he had to do in order to honor the gifts so graciously given him. To have the pleasure of Sara's company for as long as he could would become his goal. And if it would be God's will, it would happen.

***

The bitter and foreboding winter months eventually gave way to a kinder and more gentle season. Stark white dunes of snow melted into the soft brown soil beneath. As if awakened by an unheard whisper, green began to appear, clothing the earth's nakedness.

Sara delighted in the season's change. As each wildflower rose its head, she became increasingly interested in learning their names. After bidding her students farewell at the end of each day, she would head out of town, spending hours comparing plant life on the prairie to photos in a tattered paperback.

By now, going to the Olsons on the weekends had become routine. Once again, it was calving season. While she had doubted John's sincerity when he had bowed out on her graduation a year earlier, her questions met with an abrupt halt. Calves could come at any time, and just like a good doctor, John was always on call. On any given night, between 15 and 20 calves could be born. In most cases, the calves were dropped without any problems. But during one of her weekend visits, Sara learned it wasn't always so easy.

A smaller heifer that John had been watching closely, and moved to the yard as a precaution, went into labor about 6 p.m. Saturday night. Although Sara couldn't tell, John pointed out her nervously twitching tale and anxious pacing as a sign something was about to happen.

Three hours later, the heifer was down. Sara knew she should be getting back to town, but she was too intrigued. Around the cattle, John seemed so concerned and capable. She enjoying watching him work as much as she did seeing the outcome of the labor.

Sara gasped as she saw a delicate pink nose appear from the mother's body. John bent down and wiped mucus away. Fifteen minutes later, just one of the calf's front legs was exposed. Immediately aware there was a problem, John snapped into action, spreading out a fresh bale of straw for bedding.

The cow had laid down in a small area of the barn. Needing more room to work, John grabbed the cows hind legs. Using all his strength he pulled the limp animal into a more open area.

By the time he finished maneuvering it into position, the calf's tongue was becoming enlarged, a sign the stressful delivery was causing its head to swell. Slipping on a pair of rubber gloves, John moved into position behind the cow.

Sara crouched down behind the cow, intent on what was happening. She was flabbergasted to see John's hands, and then arms, disappear from view within the helpless mother cow. In a short time he assessed the situation and quickly removed his hands, grasping the calf and maneuvering it back into the birth canal. Straining, John floundered inside the cow for a minute before locating the calf's other front leg and directing it outward.

Once the legs were out, the rest of the calf quickly followed. Smoothly, the newborn slipped from its womb and landed with a slippery thud on the freshly-spread straw. Twisting her head upward, the exhausted mother glanced at her offspring, then laid back down, spent from her struggle to bring forth new life.

Sara reached out to pet the wet calf and was surprised at the coarseness of its fur. With great effort the new calf weakly drew in its feet. Wobbling, it soon stood on knobby, thin legs.

By then, the mother was also showing signs of recovery. John motioned for Sara to follow him and they walked behind a fenced area.

151

Pulling the gloves from his hands, John leaned toward Sara and spoke in a low voice.

"We'd better clear out. This cow is used to being in an open prairie, not around people. She may get mad and give us both a good chase," he said.

Before leaving the barn, John and Sara glanced back one last time. The new mother had found her feet and was judiciously licking at the fragile, quivering life by her side. Floundering clumsily, the youngster found his mother's udder. Cautiously, not knowing what to expect, the calf at first sucked weakly. Encouraged by the warm, soothing milk that sprang forth, it's efforts became more determined. With increasing urgency, the calf seemed to grasp greedily for the life that had almost shunned it.

Sara and John quietly left the barn, each contemplating the grace and brevity of life.

Chapter 9

The spring sun began to cast short shadows on the sandy Nebraska soil. At school, Sara noticed restlessness welling up within her students as the promise of summer swims in the Platte's cool waters became a real possibility.

She was caught up in their lighthearted attitudes and welcomed the chance to get lost in the careless revelry of youth. She delighted in the excitement the rowdy tomboy expressed as he presented her with a fat, sleepy-eyed frog. As an excuse to get outdoors, Sara put together a quick lesson plan on wind. Sara rounded up her students and spent a day making kites. Then, they watched them float, wayward birds drifting effortlessly in the heavens.

So distracted, it was easy for Sara to push away thoughts of the school year coming to an end. There were choices to be made. The time for renewing her contract was drawing near. But the struggle of choosing between her new life in North Platte and the one she left in New York left a dull ache in her breast.

Thoughts about her mother created a throbbing sense of abandonment in her heart. But struggling to understand the reasoning behind Agnes' reaction was fruitless. Each time she tried to find an answer, more questions crowded in until she felt dizzy and sickened.

Instead, she was content to watch the kites flutter timelessly in the breeze. They were so beautiful, yet so unaware freedom was unattainable. While the wind tugged them upward, it seemed ironic that what truly gave them flight rested below. A string, no bigger than a whispered promise, offered the support necessary to give flight.

Rather than struggle with the future, Sara decided she would enjoy floating awhile, like the dancing kites, enjoying the moment as long as she could. She would look forward only a few hours. It was the end of the week, and John had informed her he had a special activity planned. He would pick her up this evening, as had become their habit. But this time, he had instructed her to dress in her Sunday best.

Sara turned over the possibilities in her mind. Did a new restaurant open up that she was unaware of? Was there a special event taking place in another nearby city? Whatever John had up his sleeve, Sara relaxed, sure she would enjoy it. He had a way of making things special and she was not about to interfere by asking a lot of questions.

That evening, Sara raced to her door and opened it excitedly at John's knock. She immediately realized he was sharply dressed in the suit he had bought in New York last year. His dark black hair were parted to the side and slicked back handsomely.

John whistled softly as Sara twirled around to show off her new dress. The straight-cut A-line garment accented her figure nicely. Fashioned of midnight-blue silk, it was trimmed with a row of glittering gems. Her hair, swept into a French twist, revealed earrings that exactly matched the rhinestones adorning her garment.

"What do you think of it?," Sara said, parroting a fashion model as she walked back and forth across her living room.

"Why, you look ... stunning," John said, smirking inwardly at his word choice.

"Stunning, is it? That isn't a word I get to hear every day."

"O.K., I know there's a story here," John said, crossing his arms suspiciously. "Did you order this dress in from New York."

"Why, Mr. Olson. I would think such an accusation below you. As it so happens, I made this dress."

"You? Sewed?"

"Don't be so surprised. It so happens Mrs. Hanna, the Home Ec teacher, had pity on me. She's been giving me pointers after school. Since it sounded like you've got big plans for tonight, I thought it would be an excellent opportunity to see if it actually fits."

"Well, although beautiful, it is no match for the lovely lady wearing it. Now, if you're ready, we'd better be heading out."

Exiting her apartment, Sara was surprised at how warm the air had gotten. Still, she draped a shawl over her arm in case the evening got chilly. She was absentmindedly digging through her purse when John stopped beside a new car and opened the door for her.

Sara stood in surprise.

"What's this?"

"I decided I'd keep the miles off mom and dads and spring for one of my own. My friend Jeff is a salesman here in town and let me in on it for a pretty reasonable price. It isn't new, exactly. But its newer."

"Well, no wonder you wanted to celebrate! Let's see how it works!"

John drove out of town, heading east. They continued on for almost an hour before reaching a building surrounded with a crowded parking lot. A lit sign near the entry indicated they had arrived at a dance hall called the "Flying B."

As John led Sara into the building, they saw a large dance floor surrounded by numerous booths. Above each hung a sparkling silver globe that reflected colored lights throughout the dance hall. Women in long, flowing gowns were led by men adorned in suits. Orchestra members holding glossy horns rattled off a popular big-band number.

John and Sara were shown to a table and offered menus. After placing orders, John asked Sara to dance. Around and around they spun on the dance floor, the rhythm of the music and dancing lights an elixir intoxicating their senses.

With their meal, John ordered a bottle of wine. A break by the band opened time for some conversation.

"Well, what do you think?," John said, shoving a mouthful of prime rib into his mouth.

"I'm horribly impressed. Why haven't I heard about this restaurant? I thought teachers were the first to know about places like this."

"It just opened up about three weeks ago. Zeke tells me its been packed every weekend."

"Small wonder. It's unusual to have a place like this in Nebraska."

John slowed his chewing for a moment, then washed down his food with a gulp of wine.

"Oh, I don't know. We aren't so terribly far behind. I mean, not in the things that really matter."

Sara paused to think about what John had said and noticed he took another large drink of wine. He immediately reached for the bottle to refill his glass.

"Well, one thing is for sure, you won't fall behind on wine consumption for the evening. You must be particularly fond of this variety, because I can't ever remember seeing you enjoy alcohol quite so much."

John smiled, stuffing in another mouthful.

"You know what they say, 'Live for the moment'."

The band's intermission ended as John and Sara finished up their meals. They soon joined the others on the dance floor once again.

Time passed quickly and John indicated it was time to leave. Sara briefly hesitated, sad to leave the gay spell the place cast. But John remained insistent, helping Sara adjust her shawl.

However, instead of going out the front door, John motioned for Sara to follow him down a hallway leading to the building's rear. Stepping out into the evening air, the dance floor's smoky, sparkling gaiety quickly disappeared into the background. Replacing the glittering globes were a thousand stars. John and Sara gazed at them, convinced their winking lights were placed there especially for them to enjoy.

As Sara's eyes adjusted to the darkness, she made out the outline of several small airplanes sitting at the end of what appeared to be a runway.

"What is this place?," she asked.

"Well, if you'll recall, this place is called the Flying B. The "B" represents the owners last name. And this runway strip is where Flying comes in. Some of the people in there actually flew in for the evening."

John took Sara's hand and led her a short way down the runway. They stopped beside a man lazily smoking a cigarette and leaning against an airplane.

"Are you Cap?," John asked.

"Yep. You must be John Olson." The man lifted his sleeve, squinting to make out the numbers beneath the light of a dim street lamp located nearby. "And right on time, too. I'm ready if you are."

John nodded as Sara looked from one to the other, confused. The man called Cap walked around the side of the airplane, drew a door open and extracted a small ladder which he set up in front of the door. John followed his lead, inviting Sara to proceed first.

Hesitatingly, Sara climbed up the ladder and took a seat in the tiny plane. John squeezed in beside her. A short time later, the plane was taxiing down the runway with Cap at the controls.

"Just sit back and relax. It's a nice night and we should be in for a smooth ride. In the mood for some music?"

John nodded yes, and a second later the cabin was filled with the same smooth sounds they had listened to earlier that night. The small plane quickly gained speed, lifting effortlessly off the ground. Up they went, quickly shrouded in the rich darkness of night.

Sara snuggled into the seat, enchanted.

"My, this is quite a special surprise. This is remarkable, really. It's like we're all alone in the world when we're up here."

John reached in his pocket, just as he'd done a hundred times that night. Again, he found it — the smooth velvet box that held a single ring.

He had bought it weeks ago, sheepishly going into the jewelry store and selecting it from among many displayed within the glass case.

It had taken him forever, and he had almost left empty-handed.

But he was overcome by doubts. "What kind of foolish person am I to think a person like Sara would accept my proposal? A college-educated woman and a rancher from Nebraska?"

John struggled with the questions running though his mind at length. Finally, as he was about to leave, the jeweler remembered another ring that had arrived just that morning. A few minutes later, he returned from the back room, a small blue-velvet box in hand. Flipping it open, the jeweler lowered the eyepiece clasped to his head and critically examined the diamond for flaws. After a few seconds, he appeared satisfied and handed the open box to John.

The pear-shaped jewel within seemed to capture a hundred colors, brighter and more radiant than any of the others on display. Its unique cut and glittering beauty seemed to contain the essence of Sara's spirit. He was drawn to the gem, just as he had been drawn to Sara since the first time he met her. Hesitating, anxious, he decided to purchased the ring.

Since then, he'd taken it out many times, gazing at its perfection as a knot of anxiety formed in his stomach and caught in his throat. He had agonized over how to deliver it to Sara and in the end had painstakingly planned this evening.

He had almost backed out. Several times, the anxiety of Sara turning down his proposal rattled his nerves and undermined his confidence. To hide it, he'd thrown himself into the evening, indulging in dance and drink to keep his feelings in check.

Now, as he sat by Sara, John's remaining fears trickled away like the grains of sand in an hour glass. As he thought of the situation, the humor caught him off guard. If Sara reacted negatively to his proposal, she had little recourse. Since they were thousands of feet in the air, it would be difficult for her to leave without hearing him out.

"Actually, it did take a little planning," John hedged. "But I hope you'll think it's worth it."

"Absolutely. I love it!," Sara said, grasping John's hand as she gazed out the window.

"Well, the reason I brought you up here. Well, I wanted to do something unique. To give you this."

John reached overhead and snapped on a small overhead light. Bringing the box out of his pocket, he opened it and gave it to Sara.

For a moment, she was speechless. Without warning, tears welled up in her eyes.

"Sara, I was wondering if you would marry me. I realize this is sudden, and there are some problems in your family right now, but I wish you would consider it."

Sara remained silent, unable to fully comprehend what John was saying.

"You see, I've given this a lot of thought. And I realize it would be unfair to ask you to marry me, and expect you to spend the rest of your life in these sandhills. So, if you accept my proposal, I would be willing to give up ranching. We could move back East where you belong. I would just need to put my affairs in order and give my parents a years notice so they can find a good tenant. Then we could leave. What I'll do back in New York I don't know, but I'm not afraid of work. I'll find something.

"I love the sandhills, Sara. But I love you much more."

Sara quickly dried her eyes with her wrist.

"You'd — you'd do that for me? Why, John, I never realized ... But. Well. I mean, YES! I would be proud to be Mrs. John Olson!"

With that, Sara reached over, giving John a hug and kiss. Putting his arm around her shoulders, they leaned back into the seat, enjoying the moment. The planes gentle humm created a subtle serenade as the small plane sailed under the moonlight.

"Look!," Sara said, pointing downward.

Beneath, a hundred glittering lights twinkled gleefully. It was Lincoln, the state capital. In the distance, they made out the sower which was lit by a large floodlight. The majestic building towered above the city, a focal point for miles.

Slowly, the airplane circled around the city, John and Sara gazing down at the lighted streets. Eventually, they again turned westward, leaving the big city behind.

Sara looked at John thoughtfully.

"You know, John, you belong in the sandhills. This is what you know and have grown to love. Your parents mean a lot to you, and they've come to mean a great deal to me, as well. I could never insist that you give up all that you know and love for me. Why don't we give it a try on the ranch first, and see what happens.

"If this is where you are happy, I need to do everything I can to make our marriage happy for both of us.

"But let's leave our options open, just in case. Say we go back to New York once a year for a couple weeks. Maybe even stay with my parents, if mom calms down. Spending this time away would give each of us a chance to step back and review our lives, then do what is appropriate.

"Your love for me, John, is very important. We will make it work, whatever it takes."

After Sara and John got off the airplane, they walked to the car hand in hand. The drive home seemed long, and both were quiet as they contemplated the future.

The next afternoon, Sara and John broke the news to Ed and Helen, who were thrilled at the prospect of adding Sara to their family. When they returned to Sara's apartment, she picked up the telephone to dial her parents.

She hesitated, just for a minute. Then she quickly dialed the number and waited nervously. Relief washed over her when she heard her father's voice on the other end of the phone.

"Hello, dad. I've got some news," Sara took John's hand anxiously.

"Really?"

"Yes. It's John. He and I, I mean he proposed. And I said yes! We're going to get married! You're going to have a new son-in-law!"

"Why, congratulations, dear. Have you set a date yet?"

"No, not yet. But soon. Before fall, I think."

There was a short pause on the other end of the phone. Joe's voice took on a strained tone.

"You're mother has overheard our conversation. Would you like to speak with her?"

"Yes, dad. If you promise to pick her up after she faints."

"Fair enough," Joe said.

A moment later, Agnes' voice cut over the phone line.

"What's this I hear?," she demanded.

"John has proposed and I've accepted. We're going to get married."

"Married! My God! What in the world could you be thinking? And how do you expect to organize a wedding in New York all the way from Nebraska? It's simply beyond reason."

"Actually, mother, I was thinking we would get married here. There's a sweet little church just a few miles from where John and his family live. It will be an absolute fairy tale."

"Fairy tale is right! Surely you don't expect all of our friends to travel that distance for a wedding. No, you simply must have the wedding in New York. I'll begin the arrangements tomorrow..."

"Mother, stop," Sara said, becoming irritated. "I do not need to have the entire Hidden Valley social club at my wedding! I want it to be a small, intimate affair. Just family and a few close friends."

The phone rattled loudly.

"Mother? Mother, are you there?," Sara asked.

After a few seconds, Joe returned to the phone.

"Sara, it seems as though I'll have to make good on my promise to revive your mother. She's actually fainted dead away. I'll call you back after things have settled down."

Sara hung up the phone and smiled at John.

"Well, that went better than expected! Poor dad! I'm afraid he'll be catching the brunt of this whole thing."

John immediately became concerned.

"Sara, if you mother isn't taking things well, maybe we'd better postpone our plans. It wouldn't be a good idea to go through with getting married without her blessing."

Sara threw her head back and laughed.

"Oh, fiddle faddle. I'll have none of it. She's always tried to run my life. And for a long time, I let her. But frankly, she has nothing to say about this. And that's final."

With that, Sara and John began planning their wedding and lives together.

Eventually, they settled on a wedding day in early August. It would be hot, but well before the school year got underway. Sara made the decision to sign another one-year contract with the school. Until something more appropriate came along, they decided to live in Sara's small apartment, which would make it easy for her to continue on in her job.

Sara giggled, shocked by her lighthearted happiness. She was amazed that she felt like a school girl again herself, giddy with thoughts of the life ahead.

John was also giddy, but for quite different reasons. While he loved Sara, there was no doubt in his mind his union with her would create numerous challenges. Except for his time abroad, John had always lived with his parents. His work was just outside the door, a few steps away.

160

He was concerned about not being nearby to deal with everyday problems as they developed. When not there, the work would fall on his father and Zeke. Both had been holding their own, but John was concerned the extra stress would cause his father's health to suffer. And while Zeke was a gruff old goat, days of wear and tear on the prairie were catching up. He was beginning to walk slowly. An old knee injury was beginning to materialize. Shuffling more slowly now than in the past, his right leg trailed behind and resisted the lightheartedness of spirit.

John had faith everything would work out in the end. But anxiety still reared its ugly head, even as Sara delighted in picking out her wedding dress and fretted over decorations that would grace the small country church where they planned their nuptials.

At long last, all the arrangements were made and the wedding day was just a week away. Sara called home frequently, usually talking to her father. She learned that Agnes was still resisting Sara's decision.

Although Joe tried to make light of the situation, Sara knew from his tone that things back in New York were going badly. When pressed, Joe admitted Agnes had dropped out of the social scene. She had taken to spending time around the house, fretting over small details and driving the kitchen staff half mad. When not doing her best to patronize the hired help, she would spend her time sitting sullenly in the parlor, staring blankly in a book or out the window.

While Joe expressed dismay, he was not overly concerned about his wife's attitude.

"She will just have to buckle down and get herself together. I'm sure she'll come around," Joe said in an exasperated tone.

So it was with a partially laden heart that Sara approached her wedding day. Her father had said he was planning on attending, but, judging from his wife's attitude, he thought it unlikely she would make the trip out.

Therefore, Sara was not surprised when, one day before the wedding, Joe stepped from the train alone. He was happy and lighthearted. Sara knew his attitude was partially for her benefit, so as not to spoil her special day. However, try as she may to downplay the boycotting of her wedding, Sara was crushed. For her it was the ultimate slap in the face.

Sara knew her mother's failure to attend her wedding was part of an ongoing power struggle — a battle her mother would do anything to win. But in not attending, Sara knew things between she and her mother would never be the same. For the young girl, it was the ultimate blow; the removal of love and support that she had always enjoyed.

Sara thought these things, even as she chatted nonchalantly with her father. It was as if her body was running itself, her happy, calm exterior expertly shrouding the inferno burning her soul. On one hand, she felt pain unlike she'd ever known before. It wanted to drive her away crying wildly as tears streamed down her face.

But those emotions were balanced by the joy she felt in knowing John, the thrill she felt in being singled out for his attention and love. It was an honor she wore proudly and which would carry her into the future. A future her mother apparently did not want to be a part of.

At last, the day arrived. The family members and a few close friends entered the chapel doors, strains of music from an old organ resonating throughout. Fresh flowers, picked just that morning from local gardens, graced the altar and pew sides, sending out the fragrance of life.

Sara peeked out of a side room at the back of the church anxiously. She had asked a friend from work to act as a bridesmaid, and they busied themselves fretting with Sara's veil.

Soon, the organ boomed out, a signal to begin the procession. Sara took her place, her hand twined gracefully around her father's arm. The organ music abruptly stopped, and Sara glanced at her father with a worried expression. A few seconds later, the crisp, clear strains of a violin cut through the air. The music was lovely, at first soft and hesitant. Gradually, it got louder, singing out a smooth, yearning melody that spoke of new love and the promise it held.

Flawlessly, the soothing strains continued to tell their heartfelt tale. Unable to bridle her curiosity, Sara leaned out into the church and peeked into the choir loft above. Her mouth fell open when she saw Zeke, cleanly shaven and in his Sunday best, masterfully coaxing the violin he held into song.

Sara resumed her post, wiping a tear from her face. Never would she have imagined such beauty was held within Zeke's gruff, chew-spewing exterior. If his song relayed his feelings about Sara and John's marriage, Sara was quite sure she had never been so honored by another.

The music paused briefly, and then, on the ministers cue, the organ and violin joined together to play the wedding march Sara had selected. John was waiting at the front of the church, and Sara's bridesmaid slowly began drifting down the isle.

As Sara wiped another tear from her eye, Joe bent down to whisper into his daughter's ear.

"You're a beautiful bride. I will always wish you happiness in your life. But you will always be my little girl," he said, brushing her brow lightly with a kiss.

"And mine, as well," a voice chimed in.

Sara and Joe turned in surprise. Behind them stood Helen, her gloved hands suddenly wringing nervously.

"Why, what in the world are you two looking at? Has a ghost walked in?," Agnes said, looking from side to side in mock surprise.

"Why, mother. I, well, I thought you weren't coming."

`"What! And miss the wedding of my only lovely daughter? I would have to be a complete idiot!," Agnes said.

Walking to Sara, Agnes embraced her tightly. Again, the tears streamed down Sara's face. Agnes stepped back and looked at Sara closely.

"My goodness, look at you!," she said, opening her beaded purse and extracting a white lace-edged handkerchief. "What kind of a bride goes down the isle with her face all wet. Now here you go."

Agnes dabbed her daughters eyes with the handkerchief, then thrust the cloth into her hand.

"Here, silly. You'd better take it along just in case. Now, what are you two waiting for? Your making the groom nervous! Time to get moving."

Sara and Joe looked at each other and smiled. An usher offered his hand to Agnes, and the two proceeded to the front of the church. The bride and her father followed, Joe passing Sara's hand to John's outstretched palm.

The ceremony went without incident. Afterwards, John and Sara departed from the church amid a shower of rice. Sara turned to wave a final farewell to her guests, but found herself swept up off her feet into John's strong, capable arms. He kissed her gently, his lips brushing against her lips like a butterfly's wing. Sara closed her eyes, a flush of happiness and newfound womanhood rushing through her body. When she opened them, John was smiling down at her, love beaming from his face.

The two slid into his car and began driving away. Tinkling tin cans clattered merrily, following the car down the dusty country road. Helen, Ed, Joe and Agnes stood side by side, waving from the top of the church steps until the newlyweds disappeared from sight. Their absence hung over them, the melancholy of the past sifting despairingly with hope of a future unknown.

***

A few months after the wedding, Ed and Helen decided to leave the ranch and live in North Platte. John and Sara moved into the trusty old farm house and began to settle into their own routine.

In May, Sara completed her second year of teaching. John was relieved to see she appeared to be adjusting well to life on the ranch. After work, she would return home and set out onto the prairie with her pen, note pad and trusty bird-watching booklet. She spent hours sitting on the banks of the Platte, studying wildlife and keeping notes in her journal. To John, it seemed she had taken a real interest in the land that was so much a part of him.

But at the supper table one evening, John's secure attitude was rattled unexpectedly. Sara sat down at the table, fussed with her mashed potatoes and then laid her fork down abruptly.

"John, we need to talk," she said, her finger absentmindedly tracing the pattern of the flowered table cloth.

"I'm not going to renew my teaching contract next year."

John immediately set down his fork. Had he been wrong? Was Sara actually miserable? His mind raced as he considered making good on his offer to move back to New York if Sara so desired.

"John, for heavens sake! You look like your going to faint! Here." she said, pouring him a glass of iced tea, "You'd better take a drink."

"No, you just go ahead. I'm listening." John felt the urge to tug at his collar, which suddenly seemed tight.

"Well. As I was saying, I've decided not to sign on for next year." Raising her brows slightly, a sly grin crept over her face. "Because you, Mr. Olson, will need help taking care of your new ranch hand."

John searched Sara's face questioningly. She giggled slyly.

"A baby, silly. You're going to be a father in six or seven months."

For a moment, John felt as if he'd been kicked in the gut by a wild stallion. He could hardly believe his ears. He sat, not daring to move, as Sara's words rattled around in his head.

The silence hung there, for just a moment. With a start, John leapt to his feet and let go a loud whoop. Taking Sara in his arms, he squeezed her hard, lifting her into the air.

164

"Oh, my! I'm so sorry!," he said, placing Sara down gently.

Sara's laughter danced around the room, a tear of joy slipping down her cheek.

"You're going to be a daddy, Mr. Olson. Just imagine that!," she said, kissing him firmly on the lips.

After that, the Olson's life rapidly began to change. Knowing she could never bare to be away from her child, Sara began brainstorming ways to stay on the ranch while still bringing in a little extra money. Laying on a blanket, gazing up at the sky through the leaves of an old oak tree, Sara was suddenly hit with an idea. She loved it out here. Why wouldn't others? The longer she thought, the more excited she became. Grabbing her note pad, she frantically began jotting down ideas.

Slowly, the seeds of an idea began to take shape. A ranch. A dude ranch, or perhaps a bed and breakfast inn. Sara tapped the end of a pencil against her head absentmindedly. It should be a place where people who never had the opportunity to enjoy the sandhills, could come and enjoy them. Those who would never have the chance to enjoy watching the soft, orange sun slip below an endless horizon. People who were, in short, much like Sara.

By the time John came in for supper, Sara was bubbling over with enthusiasm. Without even pausing to take a breath, she laid out her plan. As John listened, he slowly nodded in approval, seeing the merits of her idea.

"We'd take it slow, of course. Do our research. And we'd have to build bunkhouses. And clients. I know daddy would throw some business our way. He knows tons of people and they're always looking for a novel way to spend their holidays," Sara said, breathlessly.

"Well, it does sound interesting. I think you may have something here, Mrs. Olson." John reached out across the kitchen table and squeezed Sara's hand affectionately.

"Come on, let's step out onto the porch," Sara prodded.

Together, Sara and John walked through the screen door, it's creak a familiar melody. Sara spotted a wobbly young calf struggling to suckle its mother and unconsciously laid a protective hand over her own swelling womb. In the distance, a morning dove sang out its plaintive song.

Sara looked into the distance, where land held up the endless blue sky. Here, there was no ocean, no mountains. But as she felt John's arm slip protectively around her waist, she knew this is where she wanted to be. Sara's heart told her it was home.

Printed in the United States
4113

9 780759 653856